CLIFFS
OF FALL

═══════════

and Other Stories by

SHIRLEY HAZZARD

PICADOR
FARRAR, STRAUS AND GIROUX
NEW YORK

CLIFFS OF FALL. Copyright © 1961, 1962, 1963 by Shirley Hazzard. All rights reserved. Printed in the United States of America. No part of this book may be used or reproduced in any manner whatsoever without written permission except in the case of brief quotations embodied in critical articles or reviews. For information, address Picador, 175 Fifth Avenue, New York, N.Y. 10010.

www.picadorusa.com

Picador® is a U.S. registered trademark and is used by Farrar, Straus and Giroux under license from Pan Books Limited.

For information on Picador Reading Group Guides, as well as ordering, please contact the Trade Marketing department at St. Martin's Press.
Phone: 1-800-221-7945 extension 763
Fax: 212-677-7456
E-mail: trademarketing@stmartins.com

Nine of the stories in this collection appeared originally in *The New Yorker.* "A Place in the Country" was first published in *The New Yorker* as two stories entitled "A Place in the Country" and "A Leave-Taking." "In One's Own House" appeared in *Mademoiselle.*

Library of Congress Cataloging-in-Publication Data

Hazzard, Shirley, 1931–
    Cliffs of fall and other stories / Shirley Hazzard.
        p. cm.
    Contents: The party—A place in the country—Vittorio—[etc.]
    ISBN 0-312-42327-6
    EAN 978-0312-42327-8
    I. Title.

PR9619.3.H369C55 1988
823

88-17970

First published in the United States by Alfred A. Knopf, Inc.

First Picador Edition: July 2004

10 9 8 7 6 5 4 3 2 1

CLIFFS

OF FALL

ALSO BY SHIRLEY HAZZARD

Fiction
The Great Fire
The Transit of Venus
The Bay of Noon
People in Glass Houses
The Evening of the Holiday

Nonfiction
Greene on Capri
Countenance of Truth
Defeat of an Ideal

In Memory of
Elena Vivante

CONTENTS

The Party　　3

A Place in the Country　　16

Vittorio　　62

In One's Own House　　83

Villa Adriana　　107

Cliffs of Fall　　116

Weekend　　140

Harold　　152

The Picnic　　166

The Worst Moment of the Day　　177

CLIFFS

OF FALL

THE PARTY

THE Fergusons' door opened on a burst of light and voices, and on Evie's squeal of surprise—quite as if, Minna thought, we had turned up uninvited. Evie kissed her.

"Our shoes are a bit wet," said Theodore. He stood aside to let Minna enter. "Is that all right?"

Evie had slanting eyes, and a flushed, pretty face. She was wearing a shiny brown dress, and her hair bubbled down her back in fair, glossy curls. She had an impulsive way of embracing people, of holding them by the hand or the elbow, as though she must atone for any reticence on their part with an extra measure of her own exuberance— or as though they would attempt to escape if not taken into custody.

"Minna, what a beautiful dress. How thin you are. Theodore, you never look a day older, not a single *day*. I expect," she said to Minna, "that he is really very gray— with fair people it doesn't show. He'll get old quite suddenly and look like Somerset Maugham." She gave Minna

3

a sympathetic, curious look from her tilted eyes. (Minna could imagine her saying later: "I never will understand why *that* keeps going, not if I live to be a hundred.") "Here's Phil."

Evie's husband came out of the living room, a silver jug in one hand and an ice bucket in the other.

"You look like an allegorical figure," Minna told him.

Phil smiled. He went through life with that sedate, modest smile. He was a corporation lawyer, and he and Evie had been very happy together for fifteen years. Long ago, however, at his own expense and to everyone's surprise he had published a small book of love poems that carried no assurance of being addressed to her. "What would you like to drink?" Phil asked. "Minna, come into the kitchen and help me with the ice. Otherwise I'll never get a chance to talk to you."

Evie was leading Theodore away. Minna looked apprehensively at his straight back as it receded toward a group of people in the living room. He will enjoy himself, she thought, and then reproach me for letting him come.

In the kitchen, Phil's eleven-year-old son was emptying ash trays into a garbage pail.

"Hello, Ronnie," Minna said. She turned on the cold tap for Phil.

"Oh hullo," Ronnie said, intent on his work. "Alison's got the virus." Alison was his sister.

"But not badly," said Phil. "Thank you, Minna, I think that's about enough."

4

"I got her a card," Ronnie said.

"How nice," said Minna, breaking up a tray of ice.

"It says 'Get Well Quick.' "

"That sounds a trifle peremptory."

"I expect the sentiment counts for something," Phil observed from the sink.

"Taste is more important than sentiment," Minna decided, without reflection.

"Yes, I suppose I agree with that."

She smiled. "The combination, on the other hand, is irresistible."

"You're beginning to talk like Theodore. Ronnie, you could be handing round the peanuts."

"There aren't any peanuts."

"Shrimp, then—whatever there is. For God's sake." Phil took the ice bucket from Minna and put it on a tray with the jug. They moved toward the door. "Now," he asked her again, "what would you like?"

She would have liked to stay in the kitchen with Phil and Ronnie, although the light was too bright and there was nowhere to sit down. The kitchen chairs were covered with half-empty cartons of crackers and, in one case, with a large chalky bowl in which the dip had been mixed. Ends of celery and carrot had been left on the table, together with an open container of sour cream and two broken glasses. It was, Minna decided, like the periphery of a battlefield strewn with discarded equipment and expended ammunition. When I go into the other room, she thought, I will have to talk, and listen, and be aware of Theodore across the room.

"What can I have?" she asked Phil, as they went down the corridor.

"Anything you like. There's punch, if you want that." He paused to introduce Minna to a young man and a girl with a hat full of roses.

"Minna?" said the girl. "What a pretty name."

"Her real name is Hermione," said Ronnie, coming up with a plate of shrimp.

"Preposterous name," Minna agreed. "I don't know why parents do such things."

"We called our baby Araminta," said the girl bravely.

" 'Araminta sweet and faire . . .' " Phil quoted tactfully. Minna frowned. "That's '*Amarantha*,' " she said, and wished she hadn't. She and Phil edged past, and found themselves at a long table, beside a bony man in black and an opulent, earnest woman in purple. "Punch would be lovely," Minna said to Phil.

"A Browning revival," said the man in black. "Mark my words—I forecast a Browning revival."

The purple lady sighed. "Ah. If only you're right."

"Then you do like Browning?"

"Of course. *Pippa Passes*. And I've always adored *The Rose and the Ring*."

The bony man looked disappointed. "That's Thackeray. You mean *The Ring and the Book*."

"I mean the one with the marvelous illustrations."

"Rather weak, I'm afraid," Phil said, handing Minna a

full glass. "All the ice seems to have melted." He helped someone else to punch and turned back to her. "Well, Minna—we hardly ever seem to see you. Are you very busy? Are you happy? *How* are you?"

"Oh, I'm well," she said, and could not prevent herself from looking toward Theodore. He was standing not far from her, leaning his shoulder against the wall and talking to a plump man with a beard.

The bearded man looked cross. "My dear sir," he said in a loud voice, "this is not just *any* Rembrandt. This is one of the greatest Rembrandts of all time."

"Take *Sordello*," the bony man was insisting. The woman in purple gazed at him with rapt inattention.

The girl with the roses in her hat was still standing in the doorway by her husband's side. I should go and talk to them, Minna thought; they don't seem to know anyone. All the same, they looked quite contented. She glanced round at Phil, but Evie had just come up to him with a question; she laid her hand on his arm—beseechingly and not in her public, clamorous way—and he put his head down to hers. Minna set her glass on the table. Theodore, smiling broadly, had turned away from the man with the beard. She exchanged a glance with him, and wondered what his mood would be when they were alone.

"Have you looked in the refrigerator?" Phil was saying. His head remained lowered to Evie's a moment longer. Minna looked away, as if she had seen them embrace.

The girl by the door was laughing now, the roses shaking on her hat, and the man beside her was leaning against the doorframe and smiling at her.

Minna took up her glass again and turned it in her hand, and went on watching them—with admiration, as one might watch an intricate dance executed with perfect grace; and with something like homesickness, as if she were looking at colored slides of a country in which she had once been happy.

"I behaved rather well, didn't I?" he asked. "All things considered."

She came and knelt beside his chair and kissed him. "Admirably," she said. He put his arm about her but she disengaged herself and settled on the floor, leaning against his legs. "It wasn't so bad, now, was it?"

"You sound just like my dentist." He stretched back in his chair, his palms resting on his knees and the fingers of his right hand just touching her hair.

The one lighted lamp, at his elbow, allowed them to see little more than each other and a pale semicircle of the rug on which she sat. She lowered her head and watched the bright shine of his shoe, which was half hidden by a fold of her dress. Outside their crescent of light, beyond the obscured but familiar room, the cold wind blew from time to time against the windows and the traffic sounded faintly from below. During the day there had been a brief fall of snow and, frozen at the window ledges, this now sealed them in. She tilted her head back against his knees. "It's so nice here," she said, and smiled.

He passed his hand round her throat, his extended fingers reaching from ear to ear. Her hair spread over his sleeve. "Minna dear," he said. "Minna darling."

She suddenly sat upright and raised her hand to her head. "I've lost an earring. It must be at the Fergusons'."

"No, it's here," he said. "In the other room. On the table beside the bed."

"Are you sure?"

"Positive. I remember noticing it. I meant to mention it before we went out."

"I must have looked odd at the party." She settled back again. "What was I saying?"

"How nice it was."

"Oh yes. How nice."

"Just because we haven't quarreled today."

"More than that. You've been quite . . ."

"Quite what?"

"Sweet to me."

"Not something I make a habit of, is it, these days?" His fingers were tracing the line of her jaw. "I really thought you wouldn't come today. After last week."

"We had to go to the party," she said.

"That hardly seemed sufficient reason. I thought, She won't come—why should she? There's a limit, I thought. All morning, I sat here thinking there was a limit."

"And drinking," she added, but pressed her hand, over his, against her neck.

"Well, naturally." He yawned. "God, that awful party."

"It wasn't so bad," she said again.

9

"The Fergusons are dull."

"I like Phil."

"Evie, then."

"Well. . . . But she's a good person."

"Good? I'm beginning to wonder if it's a virtue to be good. It seems to be the cause of so much self-congratulation among our friends. The sort of people who were there tonight—who choose a convenient moment to behave well and then tell themselves how sensitive they are, how humane."

"But isn't that all one can hope for? And what *is* virtue, if not that?"

"Oh—something less conscious, I suppose; something more indiscriminate. Less egotistical, more anonymous. Like that brotherhood in Italy whose members still hide their faces under masks when they assist the poor."

"I thought that was to protect them from the Plague."

"Don't be irritating. What I mean is, our good seem to be so concerned with themselves, so clubby, not mixing with the natives. Do you think those people tonight would ever make allowances, for instance, for those who want to live differently, or more fully, or risk themselves more?"

So he, too, is only concerned with himself, she reflected.

"Why, even religion—even the law, than which, after all, *nothing* could be more unjust—takes account of extenuating circumstances. But these people exclude anyone who doesn't meet their particular definition of sensibility. I'm not sure that I don't find it as distasteful as any other form of intolerance."

"I suppose they think that anyone can be kind."

"That's like saying 'Anyone can be clean' in a city where most houses don't have running water. And in the end the well-meaning people seem to do more harm than the others, who make no pretensions. Don't you think?"

"Not entirely," she said, with faint irony.

"Now you are only thinking of yourself. That's the sort of thing that makes it impossible to have any real discussion with a woman. No matter how abstract, how impersonal the subject, they will always manage to connect it in some way to their love affairs."

They were silent for a moment. She rested her hand on one of the thick, embossed Chinese roses of the rug. "Would you rather not have gone, then, tonight?"

"Infinitely."

"You only had to say so."

"You couldn't have gone alone."

"I could."

"All right, you could—but you'd have sulked for days." He turned her face slightly to him. "You're practically crying as it is."

"I always look that way."

"When you're with me, at any rate." He let his hand drop. "There were women with hats on at the party. And young couples who talked about their children. Oh, and an old lunatic who wanted to revive Swinburne."

"Browning," she said.

"Browning—was that it? So it was. Then there was Evie, of course, feeling sorry for you because of me. Because I'm so disagreeable." He laughed. "At least, it wasn't as bad as the last party they had—someone actually *sang* at that, if you remember."

"I do remember. Yes."

"And you played the piano."

"Yes."

He smiled pleasantly at the recollection. "You were terrible," he said.

"Was I?"

"Darling, you always play so badly—didn't you know that?"

"I didn't know you thought so," she said, reflecting that the knowledge must now be with her permanently. She sighed. "Theodore, why do you have to do this?"

"Why?" He looked over her head for a moment, as if the question arose for the first time and required consideration. "For that matter, why anything? Why are you here? And why is your earring in the other room? Why, in fact, do you allow this to continue?"

"Eventually, I suppose, I won't." Her voice had taken on a conversational note. "A matter of will power, probably—of making oneself want something else."

"Perhaps you don't even know what else to want."

"I think I might rather like to come first with someone —after themselves, of course. And it does seem a waste, this love, this thing everyone needs, this precious commodity—it could be going to someone who would use it properly."

"Perhaps, then, *that's* all you want? Someone to give love to—a sort of repository?"

"Perhaps. No, something more reciprocal. Only, starting over again in love is such a journey—like needing a holiday but not wanting to be bothered with packing bags and making reservations. So much trouble—being charming and artful, finding ways to pretend less affection than one feels, and in the end not succeeding, because one doesn't really profit from experience; one merely learns to predict the next mistake. No, I just can't be bothered at present." She shifted her weight and, turning, laid her arm across his knees. He bent forward and smoothed the hair back from her forehead. "So there you are," she told him. "It's all a question of inertia. I stay because leaving would require too much effort."

"Yes, I see," he said, his hand still on her head. "Of course."

"But as I say," she continued, "it's an effort one must make eventually. Simply in order to stay alive. Like going to that silly party." She plucked a thread off her sleeve. "Darling, I think I'll go home. There's no sense in this."

"That dress picks up everything," he said.

Their eyes met. She looked away, with a slight smile. "I suppose there would be a humorous side to all this, wouldn't there, if one were not involved?"

He still watched her and did not smile. "No, there would not." He leaned back again, his hands resting on the arms of the chair.

This physical detachment made her suddenly conscious that she was kneeling. She sat back on her heels. "I'm going home," she said again. She hesitated for a moment. When he said nothing, she pressed her hands on his knees and stood up stiffly.

"You must hurt all over," he remarked, getting to his feet.

"More or less."

He switched on another lamp. The light fell on heavy curtains, and on books, chairs, and a sofa.

Standing before a mirror, she drew her hair back with her hand and watched his reflection as he moved across the room. "My earring," she said.

He came back with it in his hand, and with her coat over his arm. She refocused her eyes to her own reflection in the glass, examining her appearance uncertainly as she fixed the little gold loop to her ear.

"I suppose you're right," he said, "about the way you look. You do have a rather mournful face. Not tragic, of course—just *mournful*."

"That sounds more discreet, at least." She turned and faced him, and reached out a hand for her coat. "I must go," she said.

"And the dress doesn't help—I'm not sure that black suits you, anyway. Now you really are going to cry."

"You should be trying to build up my confidence," she said, unblinking, "instead of doing everything to demolish it."

He helped her into her coat. "Confidence is one of those things we try to instill into others and then hasten to dispel as soon as it puts in an appearance."

"Like love," she observed, turning to the door.

"Like love," he said. "Exactly."

A PLACE IN THE COUNTRY

"TRY to keep the poetry separate," said May. "The rest can be arranged later." She made her way around the boxes of books and china to the doorway, and called up the stairs. "Clem! When you're finished up there, you could help Nettie with the books." She had a powerful, almost insistent voice and she evidently assumed that her husband heard her, for she came back into the living room without waiting for his reply and knelt down on the rug beside Nettie. "I can make a start on the china."

"Is Shakespeare poetry?" asked Nettie, peering into a box.

"No, he belongs with the set of Elizabethan dramatists —the old leather ones. But let Clem lift the heavy books." May was uncoiling newspaper from around a jug. Her broad, tawny head was lowered over the china into a shaft of sunlight, and its brilliant color made her actions seem less businesslike than usual. "Dreadful to think this will all have to go back to town in the autumn. Still, I'm glad we came early this year, in spite of the cold. And perhaps Clem can take long weekends when the summer comes, and be less in town. It's hard on him to travel so far for just the two days. And you, too, Nettie, now that you're living in town. Don't forget—whenever you like, Clem can drive you up for the weekend."

"Thank you," the girl said. She had filled the lowest shelf of the bookcase and now sat back on her heels to survey it.

"Nettie, are you all right?"

Nettie blew some dust off *A Shropshire Lad* and looked at May over the end of the book. "Yes, of course."

"You seem a bit pale." May lowered her voice slightly. "Aren't you well? Would you like an aspirin?"

"I'm fine. Really." Nettie turned back to the shelves with a load of books. She had rolled up the sleeves of her heavy blue sweater, and her thin forearms were grubby from the books. An imprecise black pigtail dangled between her hunched shoulders.

May eyed her for a moment with determination rather than concern, but was distracted by steps on the stairs. "Here's Clem, anyway. He can fill the top shelves."

"What is it I'm supposed to do?" her husband asked—apparently as a formality, since he went straight to the books and began stacking them on upper shelves. "Why on earth Meredith? . . . And *Galsworthy*—Oh, for God's sake, darling." He turned round to May with a book in his hand.

"Dear, I'll be here for almost six months, you know. Mostly with just the children."

"No reason to lose your head completely." He placed the book alongside the others. "Who was that on the telephone?"

"Oh, the Bairds are back—that was Sarah. They opened their house last week. Sent you their love. I asked them for dinner tomorrow night."

"I thought you had to collect Matt from your mother's tomorrow." Their elder boy was spending a few days at his grandmother's, thirty miles away.

"I'll be back before dinner. And Marion can have everything ready—I've asked her to stay a little later tomorrow evening."

Clem grunted. Nettie had only completed the two lowest shelves, and he was already stooping to fill the middle of the bookcase. He was tall and light on his feet and looked less than his age, which was forty-two. He had an air of health and confidence as he handled the books, lifting them from the box, glancing at their titles, and ramming them quickly along the shelves. He, too, had rolled up his sleeves, and his arms as they moved back and forth contrasted with Nettie's fragile and ineffectual ones.

"Here's Byron," he said, handing Nettie a book. He looked down at her for the first time, and pulled on her plait of hair. "What's this floppy thing?"

Self-consciously, she put up her left hand, the book in

her right. "I haven't had time to do it properly." They resumed their work.

I suppose, Nettie thought, as she made a space between two books and fitted Byron into it, that I am in love with Clem. Love is so much talked and written about, you might expect it to feel quite different; but no, it does correspond to the descriptions—it isn't commonplace. More like a concentration of all one's energies. There seems to be a lot of waiting in it, though. I am always waiting for Clem to come into a room, or for other people to go out: Clem, whom I've known all my life and who is married to my cousin May. (Her hands, patting the books into an even row, trembled.) I've been close to him a thousand times, and this is the first time it has made me tremble. Would I have discovered that I loved him, if he hadn't drawn my attention to it? And is that really only a week ago?

Now Clem, too, had to kneel, and her cheek came level with his shoulder. He smiled at her, a brief, open smile. Nettie reached up, still pushing the books into line, and the sweater rose above her skirt, showing a white, ribbed strip of her skin.

May rose, and took up a stack of plates. "There. I'll leave these in the kitchen and Marion can wash them later, with the lunch dishes." She moved across the room and out of the shaft of sunlight. Her back looked, once more, entirely businesslike. She had a slow, deliberate way of walking—as if she had once been startled into precipitate action and had regretted it. It was the walk of a woman who dealt with men in a straightforward way and must suffer the consequences. Her steps sounded down the uncarpeted corridor.

Clem got to his feet and rummaged in the last box. "What are these?" He held up a book he did not recognize.

"Those are mine. I thought I'd leave them for the summer. I'll take them up to my room." Nettie got up, wincing, and rubbed her knees.

He pulled the books out one at a time, flicking open the front covers. "Annette Bowers. . . . Annette Bowers. . . . A. Bowers. . . . Annette Bowers." He brought them to her, stacked between his palms, and put them into her grasp without releasing them. "Annette Bowers. I love you."

"No."

"*Yes*, I tell you," he said, shaking his head and widening his eyes in imitation of her. "Did you know that—somewhere in India, I think—there are people who shake their heads as a sign of assent, instead of nodding them?" Without lowering his voice, he went on: "What have you thought about all week?"

"You," she said gravely, with her hands about the books.

He leaned forward and kissed her brow. "Now, take your books upstairs, there's a good girl," he said.

She walked past him and out of the room.

"Oh, Clem, help her," May said, coming from the kitchen and passing Nettie in the corridor.

"I can manage," said Nettie.

May came back into the living room and sat down in an easy chair. She crossed her legs and lit a cigarette. "Do you think Nettie's all right?" she asked Clem.

He was piling the abandoned wads of newspaper into an empty carton. "Why not?" he asked.

"Oh, sometimes she seems such a . . . waif. Perhaps we should do more for her, now she's living away from home."

He had fitted the empty boxes, ingeniously, one inside the other. "We have our own lives to lead," he said.

May left early in the morning. Having meticulously calculated time and distance on a piece of paper, she could tell the hour at which she would reach her mother's house, how long she must, in order not to seem hurried, linger over lunch there, and when she and Matt might reasonably be expected home. Seated neatly dressed at the wheel of the car, she gave an impression of carrying away with her all the order and assurance of the house.

Nettie, untidy in a dressing gown, received last instructions with a series of nods whose very frequency betrayed inattention. May has our day all planned, she thought, as well as her own. She has allowed for everything except what will happen. The engine started, and Nettie waved. When the car disappeared, she turned back to the house abruptly, dissociating herself from Clem.

"Can we play dominoes?" asked Kenny, the younger boy, who had been left in her charge.

"When I'm dressed," she said.

"Doesn't it seem a pity," Clem said, "to waste a day like this inside?"

"We could go for a walk along the beach," said Nettie, still addressing herself to Kenny.

"I'd rather play dominoes."

"All right, let's play dominoes first. We *could* go for a walk after lunch."

While they played dominoes, the day deteriorated. They sat down to lunch with a Sunday halfheartedness, Clem short-tempered from not having had his way and Kenny petulant from having had his. Marion, the maid, came and went between the kitchen and the dining room, as though they were, all three, fractious children who needed supervision. The cold meat that had seemed a good idea in the morning now simply contributed to the day's feeling of being left over.

After lunch, Nettie proposed again the walk that now nobody wanted, and out of sheer perverseness they walked on the deserted beach. Nettie wore a raincoat and Kenny a waterproof jacket with a broken zipper. A wind had come up, releasing little swirls from sand that had been tightly packed all winter. The sky hung over the low-lying land, huge as a sky in a Dutch painting. Clem could not light his cigarette, although he persisted in trying. Nettie struggled to fold the flapping triangle of her scarf over her hair. After she had accomplished this, Kenny put his hand in hers, but when Clem took her hand on the other side the child pulled away and ran ahead of them down the beach.

"Children know everything," Nettie said.

"Well, they have a kind of insight into fundamentals. I don't think one can call that knowledge." He would not let her withdraw her hand from his. "You look such an orphan in that raincoat."

"I always look a bit like that, apparently."

"That's what May said."

"What did she say?"

"That you looked a waif. That we should do more for you."

"What did you say?"

"I looked preoccupied and said we had our own lives to lead."

Freeing her fingers at last, she put both her hands in her pockets and they walked a little way in silence.

He looked at her, faintly amused. "What should I have said?"

"I don't know. Did you mean that when you said it? I mean, what did you feel?"

"You'd be happier if I had felt a liar and a hypocrite?"

"That, at least, would be a redeeming feature."

He shrugged. "I rather thought I'd redeemed myself by telling you about it." He was a little bored. "I see no object in hurting people unnecessarily."

"It would be all right if it were necessary?"

"You say all the wrong things," he observed. "You have no experience—you're thrown back on your intuitions, like Kenny. That's why you make these judgments on yourself and others."

She spread her hands, distending the pockets of her raincoat. "I'm afraid of this. Of not knowing what will happen next."

"Ah, well," he said, offhandedly, "you would have come to some things pretty soon in any case, if only out of curiosity. As for the other things, you simply attract them by worrying about them. What you fear most will happen to you—that is the law."

No one had spoken to her in this way before, and for a moment she actually imagined the words sternly inscribed in a statute book. Now Clem thrust his hands into his pockets, which had the effect of making Nettie, repudiated, distractedly bring out her own.

"Watch for shells!" Kenny roared from the horizon.

Neither of them replied. Presently Clem laughed and looked at her, and touched her shoulder with his. "You're a fool," he said, more kindly.

"But what have I done wrong?"

"You got born twenty years too late."

So immense and so complex did the gulf between them appear to her that it was a shock to have it simply stated as a matter of bad timing on her part. She had once been told that the earth, had it been slightly deflected on its axis, would have had no winter; and the possibility of a life shared with Clem appeared to her on the same scale of enormity and remote conjecture. Inexperienced, as he had pointed out, she had no means of knowing if his remarks were excessively unfeeling. She knew him in his daily life to be a reasonable man; from ignorance, she assumed that his conduct now would represent the same proportions of logic and compassion.

"Let's go back," he said. He cupped his hands and shouted to Kenny. Of Kenny's response, only the word "shells" could be distinguished. They retraced the pattern of their steps on the sand, the wind now at their backs.

"The Bairds are coming for dinner," Clem remarked.

"I met them once, last year."

"Vernon is rather a bore, but I like Sarah. She has the most beautiful eyes I've ever seen." He glanced round to be sure that Kenny was following.

Nettie, annoyed, said nothing. Her dim recollection of Mrs. Baird became tinged with antagonism—a plump, middle-aged woman bullied by her husband.

"I have never heard her say an unkind thing," Clem continued, "about anybody."

Nettie reflected that this, when said of a woman, made her sound totally uninteresting.

"You can entertain Vernon at dinner," Clem said.

"How?"

"Simply by listening to him, I should think. He likes shy young things. Although you're not exactly shy, are you? It's rather as though you were afraid we might all find out what you think of us." They climbed up a bank onto the road. "I wish we were alone," he said, as though their entire conversation had been irrelevant. He opened a gate and held it for her.

"There's Marion," Nettie said.

Marion had come out of the house and was standing in the drive. She put her hands to her mouth and shouted to them.

"She can't be collecting shells, too, can she?" Clem made a gesture of not hearing, and Marion shouted again. This time, as in the case of Kenny, one word only was distinct.

"The damned telephone," he said. "You bring Kenny. I'll go ahead."

Nettie waited by the gate for Kenny, who was walking —inexplicably—backward. Clem had disappeared into the house. Marion stood by the door, holding it almost closed against the wind. When Nettie came up the steps, Marion still grasped the doorknob—as if, Nettie thought, one could not enter the house without first being brought up to date on its contents.

"Matt has a temperature."

"Is that May on the phone?"

"Yes. They can't drive back today—Kenny, turn round at once or you'll fall over something—Matt has a temperature of a hundred and two."

Nettie dressed for dinner with great care. Instead of bending hurriedly before the speckled mirror above her chest of drawers, she propped the mirror by the bed, in the strongest light, and sat in front of it. She combed her hair and wound it into a circle at the back of her head and fastened it there. She brushed the shoulders of her black dress, and clasped a string of pearls around her neck, and put on high-heeled shoes. When she was quite ready, she sat once more on the bed and took her hair down, and put it up again in the same way.

As she came downstairs, the hallway was cold from the passage of night air. The Bairds had arrived. Sarah Baird had let Clem take her coat and was standing at the foot of the stairs in a dark-blue dress; her eyes, shining from the brief drive, were very fine indeed. Vernon looked up as Nettie joined them. From the slight surprise in his face, Nettie thought that she had been right, after all, to do her hair a second time.

"Ah, here she is," Clem said.

Sarah turned and, although they scarcely knew each other, kissed Nettie. So did Vernon. "Are you warm enough in that dress?" Sarah asked her.

"It's wool," said Nettie, speaking for the first time.

Clem put away Vernon's hat and shut the closet door. "There's a fire in the living room," he said. He laid his hand lightly on Nettie's shoulder as they moved away.

Clem poured out drinks, and they sat down by the fire. Clem rattled the ice in his drink and talked about Matt's temperature. He had been trying to telephone May all evening; the telephone, on a party line, was being used.

"You must tell them it's an emergency," Sarah began indignantly.

Nettie, leaning back in a deep chair as the others bent

forward to the fire, reflected that Matt's temperature was, socially, a godsend to them all. Sarah, it seemed, moved with complete ease among children's temperatures, virus infections, the possibility—not to be ruled out—of measles. Briefly, she took charge of the conversation. "Try not to worry," she said, implying that one must by all means worry, though possibly not to distraction. The Bairds had four children, all of whose temperatures had, at one time or another, considerably outclassed Matt's.

She really is quite stupid, Nettie decided, believing—erroneously—that fine eyes could not atone for stupidity. Looking away from Sarah, she was disconcerted to find Vernon watching her. If he were capable of interpreting her scrutiny of Sarah, she wondered, would he mind? Or was it just that he took an interest in other women? But his interest gave the impression of being so general that it almost amounted to fidelity. And immediately she asked herself, "Is Clem like that? Has he done this before? Will he do it again?" The last of these questions pained her so much that she left all of them unanswered. Of course with Clem it was not the same at all, utterly different, the comparison was meaningless. . . . But in what way different?

"I know what's different," Vernon said suddenly. "You've changed your hair since I last saw you."

"And since I last saw you," said Clem, turning a little to smile at her. She thought that his tenderness, after the day's indifference, was like a warning.

"Clem could try the telephone again," Vernon said, "before we sit down to dinner."

When Vernon pushed Nettie's chair in to the table, he rested his hand, as Clem had, briefly on her shoulder. It troubled her to sit in May's place, and for that reason she took no responsibility for the meal, allowing the dishes to pass without offering to serve them, behaving as less than a guest. She was grateful to Vernon for requiring—as Clem had predicted—nothing more than a hearer. He seemed content that she should stare down onto the polished table beside her plate so long as her head was slightly inclined toward him. Once, she looked up, and Clem, who was talking to Sarah, lifted his eyes. Studying the table again and tracing the grain of the wood with her finger, she thought there had been no intimacy in his look, only a reflection of her own preoccupation, and a sort of recalcitrance. She felt that she could not breathe properly, and she disappointed Vernon by uttering a sharp sigh. The tabletop bore the damp mark of her lifted finger.

"Of course, I'm an incurable romantic," Vernon was saying. He made it sound like a disease.

"Of course," she said.

After dinner, they went back to the fire. The living room was furnished, as rooms in summer houses often are, with the mistakes and discards of a town apartment. Unabashed, these had assumed a certain style of their own. The rug was a deep cocoa color, worn pale and thin near the door and by the sofa. The chairs, with one or two defections, tended toward dark green. There was a mosaic coffee table, made by a relative, and two ash trays that had seemed a good idea one hot afternoon in Cuernavaca. The same rash expedition to Mexico was responsible for a black and brown painting in which a man and woman stared at each other with unmistakable resentment.

When the telephone rang, Clem put his coffee cup and saucer down on the uneven mosaic, where they rocked a little, and went into the hall. They heard him speaking loudly, as people do on a long-distance call even when the connection is good.

"He doesn't sound alarmed," said Nettie.

Sarah said: "One never knows. With these things."

Clem's voice went on, with long pauses. Instinctively they watched the doorway, but it was Marion, not Clem, who first appeared there, startling in a coat and hat. She gave a polite but meaning glance at Nettie, who with a little gasp of recollection sprang up from her chair and left the room.

In the drawer of the hall table there was an envelope that May had marked "Marion," and this Nettie now passed on stealthily. "I hope it's right," she said, having no reason to doubt it.

Marion, infinitely more assured than Nettie, put the envelope in an immense black handbag. "I'll be over to-morrow," she said. "And I hope Matt's all right."

"Yes. Thank you. Good night," said Nettie. She closed the front door. Clem, sitting on the stairs with the telephone receiver in his hand, was still talking, but with a terminal inflection. As she passed him, he reached out and touched her dress. Matt must be better, she thought.

When she came back into the living room, Vernon was

leaning forward as if he had been speaking earnestly. Sarah, Nettie noted, look confused. Nettie did not sit down, but started to assemble the empty cups on a tray.

"Let me help," Sarah said, taking up the coffeepot.

"Don't bother, really. I'll just leave them in the kitchen." Nettie was halfway to the door.

"Matt is better," said Clem, appearing in the doorway. "It's a throat infection, apparently."

"I knew it," Sarah said.

"His temperature is down."

"I'm so glad." The coffeepot waggled slightly. "Perhaps I should have spoken to May. What is she planning to do?"

"She's going to call me in the morning. It depends how he is—she may stay there a day or two."

Nettie took a firmer grip on the tray and walked on down the corridor. "Be careful," she said over her shoulder to Sarah, who at once followed her with the coffeepot. "There's a step." She pushed open the kitchen door with her elbow. "Can you find the light? On the left. Thanks." The light fell, dazzling, on aluminum saucepans and a huge white refrigerator. "Just put it anywhere. I'm not going to wash them tonight."

Sarah kept the coffeepot in her hands, but came across the room. "Nettie," she began, with as much solemnity as haste would allow. "We would be so pleased if you would come home with us."

Nettie put the tray down carefully by the sink. Taking up the sugar bowl, she walked past Sarah and put it away

31

in a cupboard. "Because of the ants," she remarked apologetically. She returned to the sink and started to pour away the dregs from the cups. "I don't understand," she said. Blankly, she felt this to be true. It was her own stillness she did not understand.

Sarah came and stood at the sink, so that it was impossible not to look at her. She had a flushed, uncomfortable expression and Nettie noticed that her eyes were not only pretty, but even kind. "No, of course. But Vernon feels— People around here gossip so. Unprincipled, really. You shouldn't be exposed to that." Sarah grew impatient before Nettie's empty look. "And, of course, we'd love to have you." Her voice ran down.

It is really quite easy to have the advantage over people, Nettie thought—if you can be bothered. You just have to keep quiet and look at them. "I'll have to see what Clem thinks," she said at last. She finished stacking the rinsed dishes and dried her hands. She exchanged a hopeless little smile with Sarah. "You go ahead," she said. "I'll put the light out. Watch the step."

In the hall, she stopped to straighten a mirror. She felt that she had unlimited time at her disposal. She could hear voices raised in the living room, and for a moment stood still with a child's pleasurable horror in listening to a grown-up quarrel. She stared into the mirror, exasperated —as Sarah had been—by her own unresponsiveness; to see her feelings reflected in her face would have made them clearer to her. But here was, simply, a strained, alarmed expression made the more unfamiliar by the care with which it had that evening been powdered and embellished.

As he entered the room, she heard Clem's voice, cold and angry. "I'm afraid I don't understand."

"But don't you think . . ." Sarah's voice wavered anxiously. It was her fate that evening not to be understood.

Clem broke in. "Good Lord, she's like a daughter in this house. What an extraordinary idea. Perfectly extraordinary. In fact," his voice rose on a short, humorless laugh, "if we didn't know each other so well, I would say it was—downright insulting."

"Oh dear," Sarah said. Vernon had not said a word.

Nettie came further into the room and glanced at Clem. She saw that he had managed to be genuinely angry—angry in some way with her, too. She felt chilly, and walked past him to the fire.

There was an arduous silence. The fire flared and crumbled, and flared again. Resting her arm on the mantelpiece, Nettie stayed with her back to the room, in an attitude of unintended pathos.

"Oh, hell," said Clem, concedingly. He laughed, more encouragingly, and reached into his pocket for cigarettes.

"Why are things so complicated?" Sarah asked generally. Nettie looked round at her with compassion.

"Let's all sit down and have a brandy," Vernon suggested.

"That's a rather better idea," Clem said. "Sarah—never mind. No harm done."

She gave a nervous, relieved little laugh. "Oh, Clem.

I can't tell you how sorry—No, Vernon, of course we can't. It's so late. Clem, we must be going." Suddenly active, she discovered her handbag beneath a cushion on the sofa. "Here it is."

"Are you really leaving?" asked Clem. He took her arm. They went into the hall. Vernon followed them, but stood back at the door to let Nettie pass. They did not look at one another.

Clem was bringing coats, and Vernon's hat, from the closet. Sarah kissed Nettie again and drew on her gloves. "Be sure to let me know how Matt is." She let Clem kiss her cheek. "I do hope it isn't anything serious," she said. "Clem, dear, do forgive—"

"No harm done," he repeated. He smiled with complete good will; he almost looked pleased.

Vernon took Nettie's hand briefly and released it. He followed Sarah into the garden, and Nettie stood where he had left her, behind the open door. Clem, holding the door handle, watched them go to their car. He called good night, and waved once or twice with his free hand. Sarah called out that the grass was wet. A car door, improperly closed, was banged several times before Vernon started the engine.

When the sound of the car receded, Clem closed the front door and switched off the outside lights. He linked across the lock a small gilt chain in which May had complete confidence. Now, thought Nettie, he will hesitate and smile. Instead, he turned at once with a grave, concerned face, and took her into his arms.

They stayed this way, in silence, until Nettie drew back and leaned against the door. Clem moved forward slightly, holding her with his left arm and supporting his right on the panel above her head. "Don't shake," he said at last, speaking against her hair. "It isn't complimentary." His left arm tightened. She felt him smile. "In fact, if we didn't know each other so well, I would say it was—downright insulting."

"What a summer for roses," said May. "I've never seen anything like it." She laid her sewing on her knee, and took off her glasses, and sighed. As if to make her last remark irrefutable, she closed her eyes.

Clem, in a garden chair, glanced up from the Sunday paper. "Are you tired?" Without waiting for her reply, he folded the pages in his hand and dropped them on the grass beside him. "I don't know why we read this—nothing but advertisements, and it makes one's hands black."

"I am tired, yes," May pursued. "I was gardening all afternoon."

Anyone would think gardening was a penance, Nettie observed to herself. She was sitting on the lawn, a book open in her lap. She thought that May contrived with her exhaustion to dispirit them all. The warm afternoon, the garden, the tray of empty glasses on the grass, succeeded in conveying foreboding and dissatisfaction; even the roses seemed to threaten violence, brimming over their plots of earth or arrested, scarlet, on the white wall of the house. Love, she thought, lowering her head over her book, is supposed to be enriching; instead I am poisoned (she exaggerated to hurt herself) with antagonism. Here she caught herself up—I am being an Incurable Romantic, she thought, and smiled. And yet, when I can be with him, just see him, I am happy. And I care more for him than for myself—I suppose that is enriching. I would literally die for him—only, no one wants that; they would rather you went on living and behaved reasonably. It has all happened too quickly. I keep thinking there will be a pause, I will find the place again, get back to being as I was, but that never comes. And yet the surprising part, too, is that it doesn't make more difference. I would have thought such things made one wordly; instead, one becomes more vulnerable than ever.

Lifting her eyes from the unturned page, she could see at her right Clem's legs and the side of his chair. His clothes, the wicker chair, the very newspaper he had flung down seemed involved in his personality. *He* is not vulnerable, she reflected. One can even see that from the way he sits, or moves, or reads the paper. He does not need my good opinion, as I need his. If he loves me, it is as a kind of indulgence to both of us. I cannot trust him completely —but, after all, one would not trust *anyone* completely; it would hardly be fair to them. It is the discrepancy that hurts—that I should be so aware of him, order my life, think, speak, clothe myself for him.

"Nettie, that color doesn't suit you," May remarked lazily. "If you'll forgive my saying so."

"Oh, really?" said Nettie, in an unforgiving voice.

"You should wear more blue, with your eyes. Don't you think, Clem?"

Clem looked down at the back of Nettie's head. "What color are her eyes?" he asked.

Only Nettie laughed.

"What a tiring day," May said with a certain determination. "Let's hope there won't be a storm before you get back to town."

Clem looked at his watch. "We should leave soon, if we want to arrive before dark."

"And be sure to give Nettie dinner somewhere, or she won't eat anything."

She speaks, Nettie thought, as though I were not here.

"I generally do," Clem said. "We have dinner and then I take her home."

We have dinner, Nettie repeated to herself, and then he takes me home. Every Sunday evening of this spring and summer. Occasionally they went to Nettie's small, cluttered apartment, but more often to Clem's large and empty one. Saturday's unopened mail and newspapers lay on a little table outside the front door of the apartment, and, inside, the hallway echoed as it would not have done in winter, and smelled of floor polish. Most of the windows were closed and all the blinds were drawn. There were so many doors that two people must feel slightly unsafe until they had entered one room, closed one door behind them.

"That's all right then," May said. She yawned, but resumed her sewing. "Nettie," she began again, "why don't you bring a friend next weekend? Someone your own age. Some nice young man."

"Thank you, no," replied Nettie, turning a page at last.

"You must know some."

"Well, they are stupid."

"If you are so critical," May observed comfortably, "no one will ever love you."

"And if you're so tired," said Clem, conveying disbelief, "why do you go on sewing?"

"Darling, it has to be done, and I'd rather get on with it. I don't darn your socks for amusement, after all."

I would love to darn his socks, Nettie thought. She could not tell whether this marriage was worse than other people's, although it would have gratified her to think it was. Why do men ever marry, she wondered. I can understand that women must have something of the sort—it is our nature, she thought vaguely—but why men? (She had forgotten about the socks.) Because nothing better has been worked out? But they don't even expect anything better; the limitations are flagrantly justified, like restrictions in a war, in the interests of national security. She told herself reprovingly, It is an *institution*—but this produced a mental picture of a large brick building not unlike a nineteenth-century prison. If he and I had been married, she wondered, would it have had to deteriorate into this? May and Sarah discussed their husbands as though they were precocious children—"Clem is very handy in the house," as one might say "He hardly ever cries" or "He sleeps right through the night." Let me go on believing, she asked, looking at his canvas shoe, that love isn't merely getting along with someone. She thought that once she accepted such a compromised version of love she would never reach back again to this. (She had excessive confidence in the instructive power of experience.)

Clem's foot moved. Nettie looked up. "Here's Matt," she said.

Matt came from beyond the roses, swinging a small black box camera by its strap. He was eleven, lanky and dark, with an earnest face that reflected his mother's resolute honesty and her total lack of irony. The three on the lawn watched him approach. Unnerved by their attention, he started to speak while still at a distance. "I'm going to take a picture."

"Oh God," said Clem.

"The camera was your idea," May remarked.

"*You* wanted to give him a guitar."

"I don't want to be in it," Nettie said, closing her book.

"Don't be silly," said May.

"Who'd want a picture of her?" Matt snorted foolishly. Nettie, injured, looked away.

May sighed. "Nettie, what's wrong now? He's only teasing. You should be able to ignore that, at your age."

Nettie saw no reason to expect that what had been intolerable to her in childhood should be acceptable now.

"Daddy, *smile*."

"I don't feel like smiling."

39

"It doesn't matter. You've *got* to smile."

"Put the tray out of sight," May said.

Immobilized, they stared into the sunshine. The camera clicked. Matt came up to them, twisting the knob to the next number. "It probably won't come out—there was too much light. And Daddy moved. And Nettie looked as if she was going to cry."

"My love," Clem said, keeping his eyes on the road and slowing to let another car pass. "You mustn't."

Nettie wiped her eyes with a shredding Kleenex. She moved along the seat away from Clem until she was propped in the corner.

"Make sure that door is closed" was all he said.

If I could only think of something else, she told herself —something that wouldn't make me cry. She attempted one or two seemingly arid subjects, but they led her back to tears. It was like trying not to be sick. Unable to stay at such a distance from him, she changed her position slightly, taking her weight off the car door. "It was so awful today," she said.

"Didn't seem any worse than usual."

"Well—I suppose it's worse for me than for you." She hoped he would contest this.

"Yes, I suppose it is," he agreed.

"I don't think I can come for weekends any more." Until she spoke, she had not considered this possibility.

"Nettie," he said, irritated into using her name, "that's something you must decide for yourself." After a moment, he added with ill-timed practicality: "What would I tell May?"

"You could always tell her," said Nettie, "that I've fallen in love. With someone my own age." Almost immediately, however, she threw away this advantage and laid her hand on his knee. "Oh, Clem, what will happen?"

"Darling, I don't *know*."

"But it can't go on and on like this." His silence seemed to ask, "Why not?," and to answer it she made a little explanatory gesture with her free hand. "Without any meaning," she said. "Anything to hope for."

"But it has been like that from the beginning," he pointed out, genuinely puzzled. His eyes were still on the road. "You knew that. I never promised you anything."

She was ashamed of him for this remark. She had not intended to charge him with obligations. It also occurred to her that an obligation was not the less incurred for being unacknowledged. She took her hand from his knee (he shifted his leg slightly, as though liberated from an uncomfortable pressure), and moved back against the door.

He glanced at her. "You aren't pleased?"

"Why should I be pleased? You're not trying to please me."

"I don't like to see you so upset."

"Why shouldn't I be upset? You want it every way. When shall I be upset if not now?"

"But, Nettie, what can I say? I *am* married, I *do* have two children. May is forty-three—she can't be asked to begin her life over again."

41

"I *know*, I *know*." The Kleenex had shed some flecks of white on her eyelashes. "I don't expect—I know we can't be married." (Though we might as well be, with this deplorable conversation, she thought.) "It isn't that."

"What's in God's name is it, then?"

"I just want you to understand."

"Well of course I understand," he said crossly. "How could I help it?"

She had not thought of understanding as an involuntary acquisition. "I meant—to be kind."

"Damn it, I *am* kind," he responded, raising his voice. After a moment he said, less harshly: "Aren't I?"

"Not really, no." Sensing a passing relaxation of his annoyance, she struggled for words, as if speaking on a long-distance call with only moments to reach him. Giving this up, she turned her face toward the window and wiped her eyes again, this time with the back of her hand. I do cry rather a lot, she conceded.

The Sunday-evening traffic was heavy, and the road not wide, and they moved along slowly. From a car that had drawn level with them, a little girl was watching Nettie curiously. Clem drove for a while in silence. Eventually, he turned his head once more and said: "Look, pull yourself together. We can talk about it at dinner."

Nettie clasped her hands in her lap. "I want to go straight home," she told him, as she might have said: "I am going to die." "To my place."

Clem watched the traffic again, frowning. He allowed it to move past him, to the great disappointment of the child in the neighboring car, who was swept ahead and disappeared, still gazing at them, around a bend in the road. At the next intersection, he put his arm out to signal and turned the car off the main road.

"What are you doing?" Nettie asked, as aloof as curiosity would allow.

He did not reply. They passed, still slowly, through a shopping center and a housing development. Presently they came into a suburban street lined with trees and with large, unfenced gardens. Clem drew the car in to the curb, and switched off the engine. Two boys were riding bicycles down the sidewalk, and a man washing his car turned to look at them in the fading light. Nettie stared into her lap.

Clem put his arm along the back of the seat without touching her. "Now what's all this about?" he asked her.

She smiled faintly. "You sound like a policeman."

"But, darling, what ever is it? I only said the weekend seemed no worse than usual, and you tell me you never want to see me again."

What cowards men are, she thought. "It can't be *that* incomprehensible," she said.

His fingers touched the back of her neck. She inclined her head further, away from his hand. The tears returned to her eyes. An Irish terrier ran up to the car from a nearby garden and began to bark at them. The man washing his car called sharply: "Casey!"

"Don't cry." But this time it seemed that he said it for her sake and not his own.

"No," she said, apologetically, the tears now falling for his sympathy. "I'm sorry, I suppose it's the strain."

"Well, of course," he replied, quite gently. "Of course."

"You don't know how isolated one feels. You have so many—attachments."

"You make me sound like a vacuum cleaner." He smiled. With his other hand he lifted a strand of damp hair back from her cheek.

She went on. "Perhaps it is all ordinary—what one should expect. I have only this to go on, so I don't know. It seems terrible. Because you are—have lived longer," she emended gracefully, "you have a clearer idea of what will happen. I can't see anything but a disaster . . . if this were carried to its logical conclusion." Her voice trembled.

His hand moved patiently along the exposed slope of her neck. "Life," he remarked, "is not strong on logical conclusions. Perhaps fortunately. But I do forget about your age. Because you are the youngest of us, you are the most important. And May would agree with that." (Her position seems to have been completely reversed, Nettie noted.) "You have no experience to guide you. As you say, I know so much more."

She smiled again. " 'I said an elder soldier, not a better.' "

He turned her toward him and drew her head against his shoulder. She did not resist or relax, and he sat with his arm around her. "Are you really going to leave me?"

She sighed. "Does it look like it?"

"On the contrary. I don't know what's going on in here."
He touched her head.

"Casey! Come here!" shouted the man with the hose.

"Shall we move on before this dog loses all its illusions?"
he asked her.

"But we haven't decided anything."

"We can talk about it at dinner." He released her. She
sat up straight and put her hands to her hair. "You look
all right," he told her, starting the engine. At the sudden
sound, the dog barked again. Clem swung the car round
in the middle of the street, and they returned the way they
had come.

Now he is driving too fast, Nettie observed. She took a
mirror out of her purse. She did not look back at the
square receding gardens and white houses. We disturbed
their Sunday evening, she thought, and upset their dog.
When she lifted her head, they had already reached the
main road. "My eyes are all red," she said.

"If you want to wash your face, we could go home first."

"We may never get there if you drive like this."

"Are you frightened?"

"No, but I suppose I don't want you to get killed," she
said.

He smiled and slowed down. But when she next looked
at him, his face was very serious—very sad, she realized
with a little shock, Clem's sadness seeming far more incongruous, far less bearable, than her own. "What are you
thinking?" she asked him.

"I was thinking," he replied, "if I died, how bad it would be for you. No one would understand that you were the person most to be comforted."

The telephone bell, which had been ringing in her sleep, woke her at last. When she lifted the receiver, it continued to vibrate indignantly in her grasp, like a baby that has been left crying in the dark. She opened her eyes. The room was scarcely light, the first sun thinly outlining the drawn blinds. She tried to think who she was—she could have been any one of a dozen people.

"Hullo," she murmured, pressing the receiver insecurely against her ear and lingering over the word.

"Nettie," said Clem.

"What's wrong?" she asked at once.

Disconcerted by this abrupt understanding, he hesitated. "I'm going up to the house," he said.

"But this is Wednesday."

"I'm not going to the office. I'm going up to the house. May telephoned me late last night."

Nettie raised herself on her elbow. Her hand, holding the telephone, shook from the awkward position. "She knows, do you mean?"

"From something she said, I think so." For a moment, neither of them spoke.

"It's serious, isn't it?" said Nettie, trying to compel her own responses. They were silent again, and then she said unhelpfully: "My dear."

"I'll call you from the country," he said. "After I've talked to May."

"What will you say to her?" Her words sounded in her own ears flat and forced. I have not realized it yet, she told herself remotely, as one who after an accident watches his own blood flow and feels no pain.

"I will have to see how it is," he said.

"Do you want me to come?"

"I think not."

"Call me as soon as you can."

"Yes. Of course."

"Remember . . ." she began.

"What?"

"About my love."

"Yes."

"No one will ever love you so much."

"No, I know," he said with slight impatience, as if this were irrelevant. After a moment he added: "Yes. It has been worth it." His tone was historic, she thought, like a farewell.

She put the telephone down and lay back on the pillow. The lengthening, reddish light was already the light of a very hot day, but she shivered and drew the sheet up to her shoulders, and could not get warm. I suppose I will realize it quite soon now, she thought with detachment. He said: "It has been worth it." What has it been worth? What is to happen to me? What am I to suffer? Calamity has a generalizing effect, and as yet she could foresee her suffering only in a monumental way and not in its inexorable, annihilating detail. She considered her resources, ranging her ideas, her secrets carefully against the unapprehended future. But ideas don't supplant feelings, she thought; rather, they prepare us for, sustain us in our feelings. If I understand why I am to be hurt, then does that really mean that it will hurt me less? I know that I risked—invited—this, wounded May. I have disturbed the balance. There is balance in life, but not fairness. The seasons, the universe give an impression of concord, but it is order, not harmony; consistency, not sympathy. We suffer because our demands are unreasonable or disorderly. But if reason is inescapable, so is humanity. We are human beings, not rational ones.

She thought of Clem with a slight surprise, her predicament now seeming a thing itself, scarcely connected with him. If she instinctively wished for deliverance, it was for deliverance of an unfamiliar and pragmatic nature—much as a sailor on a sinking ship might hope to see the Coast Guard rather than his wife and children. Clem cannot help me, she thought; we are not contending with the same elements. He was amusing himself with me, really. He did not want to be inconvenienced in this way; the inconvenience will be the greatest of his burdens. (She felt this almost with gratitude, relieved of the additional weight of Clem's grief.) They will make it up. They will be very solemn with each other, and May will use words like "relationship," and they will make it up. For a while they will hold each other's hands in public, and Clem will come home from the office on time. Once she has established her advantage, May will behave admirably toward me— she will be able to watch herself behaving admirably, like a person in a play. She will expect me to behave admirably back at her, but I have loved him too much for that. Or am at too great a disadvantage. Perhaps they will send me off somewhere, for a trip. (She even considered this possibility with a certain interest, wondering where she might go and what clothes she would need.) And Clem will manage to persuade himself that that is the best possible thing, that nothing could be better for me at this moment than to go ten thousand miles and be alone. He may miss me after a while, in the one particular way, but as long as he doesn't have to see me he will be all right. She dwelt for a moment, still painlessly—almost, in fact, with a smile —on Clem's resilience. Her eyes traveled listlessly around the room. I have nothing of his, she thought, nothing he gave me—not even a photograph, and he will look different now that he has stopped loving me. I couldn't prove, if I had to, that he ever existed for me—it's like that awful story about the walled-up hotel room in Paris. I shan't be able to say his name to anyone, not even to say that I miss him. It is just as he once said, no one will be able to sympathize with what I've lost—but that sounds like a funeral: "Profound sympathy in your recent loss . . ." In any case, even if they knew about it, people wouldn't sympathize. With a thing like this, they don't sympathize unless you die. And that would be exceptional.

The sun was up now, although the room was still half

dark because of the lowered blinds. It will be hot for him on the road, she thought. If he left immediately, he will be well on the way by now. He should arrive before lunch. It is an hour since he called me, and still I feel nothing; perhaps, after all, it need not be so terrible. These things happen all the time, and people survive them; they are exaggerated in retrospect, and in literature. She closed her eyes. I have not even wept, and I always cry so easily. Perhaps I can sleep, and when I wake it will seem more distant than ever. But why am I so cold, she wondered again. Why can't I get warm? She moved her arm, which had been rigidly clasped across her body, and felt it tremble. Beneath her, the bed was like stone.

She had not even finished dressing when he arrived. She had meant, of course, to take especial care with her appearance but had slept, instead, right through the morning —probably from the exhaustion of the last few days. When she awoke, there was barely time to take her shower and put the coffee on; not even time to make her bed. It was only because his train was a little late that she managed to get into her clothes before the doorbell rang.

He had taken a train that got him to town about noon; it was the only possible one, on Sunday. The day before, when he telephoned her from the country, he had said: "I'll leave the car with May and the children." It was one of the things she had wondered about when she put the phone down, trying to discover what position he had taken with May. It had been a short and comfortless conversation, because the telephone at his summer house was on a party line. And yet, she thought, if he had something definite to tell her he could have driven to another town, called from a drugstore. She had by then passed two days of silence and suspense since he left town on Wednesday to talk to May, and the overstated nonchalance of the telephone conversation made her frantic. "But can't you tell me anything?" she cried, as he prepared to hang up. After an admonishing silence, he had said only: "When I see you on Sunday."

She finished buttoning her dress and pushed her feet into a pair of sandals before she opened the door. Her face still glistened from the shower, her uncombed hair hung down her back, secured at the neck by a frayed ribbon; these things, absurdly, were uppermost in her mind as she turned the doorknob.

Clem on the other hand, was neatly dressed in a light summer suit; his collar and tie had admirably withstood the long journey in a hot train. He seemed a little browner, and his eyes were bright and slightly reddened as though he had slept badly. He came in without speaking, and she closed the door after him. He was holding a brief case, which he put down in a corner of the tiny hall. When she turned from closing the door, he said her name, and put his arms around her with such intensity of feeling that she had no time to raise her own and stood within his embrace as if she did not submit to it. Love, however, was too strong for her, and she moved her cheek against the side of his head. I will have to know soon, she thought, what he has agreed to do.

"I left the coffee on," she said, unclasping his arms and stepping aside. She went into the kitchen without glancing at him, and turned the gas off. He came and stood in the doorway. She still could not look at his face, which she knew must explain everything to her. "Shall I make you some lunch?" she asked.

"Just coffee."

She was lifting down the cups and saucers. "If you take the coffee in, I'll bring the tray." He stood back to let her pass, and she went into the living room and put the tray on a table in front of the sofa. "Thanks. Oh, not there; that won't stand heat—yes, there, on the tile." Sitting on the sofa, she poured his coffee and her own, and they drank in silence.

"You haven't had breakfast, then?"

She looked at him now, over the rim of her cup. "I only just woke up." In case that should sound unfeeling, she added: "I was exhausted." She was suddenly reminded of her appearance. She put her cup down and raised her hand to her head. "I haven't even done my hair."

"It doesn't matter," he said.

"Let me do it while you have your coffee. It won't take a minute." She started to rise from the sofa.

"No, don't go," he said, taking her hand. She sat down again, still watching him. He held her hand in both of his for a moment, and then pressed it against his mouth and burst into tears.

She let him put his head on her breast, withdrawing her hand so that she could take him in her arms. She leaned back on the sofa, slightly breathless from his weight and from the pressure of his head, which was quite hard. In spite of the discrepancy in their ages, she felt protective—almost dispassionate—as she held him and moved her hand consolingly up and down his shuddering spine. She also regarded him with a certain amount of vulgar curiosity—she had never seen a man weep before, and was young enough to consider it a monument in her experience. In addition, she was unable to rid herself of the notion that he wept for what he was about to say. Relieved of speculation, she found herself invested, instead, with the kind of momentary self-possession that is summoned up in a doctor's waiting room. She breathed, through the salt smell of his hair, the steam of the coffee and even regretted that her cup had to get cold. Her eyes, uptilted by her attitude, rested on the pale-green wall opposite her. She reflected that in love one can only win by cheating and that the skill is to cheat first. (Having coveted neither the advantage nor the skill, however, she had no justification for disputing—as she did—the defeat that confronted her.)

He raised his head and shifted his position so that he too leaned back on the sofa, although his shoulder still pressed on hers. He held her right hand in his own, and with his left felt for his handkerchief and blew his nose.

He closed his eyes, frowning, and she could see that he was studying how to begin. She tightened her clasp on his hand and said kindly, almost politely: "Don't worry. Just tell me."

He opened his eyes and sat up a little. "How good you are," he said.

This struck her as the sort of compliment one pays to a child, to encourage its behavior in the desired direction. It comforted her not at all that her judgment of him should remain thus pitilessly detached—that she saw him, perhaps, more clearly and with less admiration than ever before. The insight was useless to her, trapped as she was in the circumstance of love. She knew that sitting there with her hands clasped about his and her eyes on his face she represented, accurately, a spectacle of abject appeal. In any case, it was a habit of hers—possibly through the fear of loss—to appear most propitiating when she most condemned.

"Nothing has been decided," he said, putting away his handkerchief with a faint air of getting down to business. "I can only tell you what we feel about it."

At the word "we," she lowered her eyes and kept them fastened to the design of interlocking fingers in her lap. Aware of having somehow blundered, he had already lost the place in his text; it was asking too much of her that she should prompt him.

After a pause, he said abruptly: "I think I told you I no longer loved my wife."

"Yes," she said.

"I only said that once, didn't I?"

"Several times," she answered, unaccommodatingly.

"Several times, then,"— he agreed, with a touch of impatience. "In any case—I see now that I shouldn't have said that. I mean, that it wasn't true."

She thought that the digressions in the minds of men were endless. How many disguises were assumed before they could face themselves. How many justifications made in order that they might simply please themselves. How dangerous they were in their self-righteousness—infinitely more dangerous than women, who could never persuade themselves to the same degree of the nobility of their actions.

"What are you thinking about" he asked her.

"Men," she said absently.

Taken aback by the plural, he stopped to assemble his thoughts once more. She was not being very encouraging, lowering her eyes and offering him monosyllables in this way. But there was no reason why she should encourage him, and he reminded himself of that; he was nothing if not fair.

"Why did you say it, then?" She looked up briefly. "If it wasn't true?"

He said slowly: "I thought it was true when I said it. I'm trying to say that I don't feel quite the same—I mean, not as I did."

She was silent, watching her fingers uncurling from his

and the tiny white dots on her blue dress waver with the trembling of her knee. The words seemed so loud that she thought their echo could diminish only over a lifetime, would go on sounding within her forever: "Not as I did." "Not as I did."

"I would always care about you," he went on, now anxious to be understood, as it were, once and for all. "But it can't be as it was. . . . I'd like to think we can go on being fond of one another, that you can think of me as someone who . . ." He paused for a moment and then continued, unconscious of irony, "who showed you what love is." He withdrew his hand from her slackened grasp and lifted her chin so that she looked at him. "Darling, please. Please try to understand."

"I do understand, I do really," she said earnestly— almost in a tone of reassurance. "It's only that I cannot bear it."

He withdrew his hand and leaned forward with a little sigh, his elbows on his knees. Having been compelled to look at him, she now could not stop doing so. When he turned back to her, he was unnerved by that intent, expectant stare. Spreading one of his palms upward on his knee in an apparent appeal to common sense, he met her eyes and said, reasonably: "My dear, we have to come to terms with this."

"Yes, to terms," she said. "But whose terms—isn't that the point?"

"*Don't.*" Bending forward again, he took a sip of his

cold coffee. "I hate to hear you talk like that." He did not know how to show her that she was simply adding, uselessly, to an already difficult situation. After a silence, he asked: "Do you have anything to drink?"

She got up and put the cups and saucers back on the tray: "Is Scotch all right?" She went into the kitchen, and in a few moments reappeared carrying a bottle and a glass full of ice. He saw that her hand shook as she set the glass on the table.

"You mustn't exaggerate the importance of this," he told her.

She let him take the bottle from her and fill the glass. "But it does seem rather important," she answered, apologetically. She sat down again and watched him drink, so obviously awaiting his next pronouncement that he took an extra sip of whisky to gain time.

"Yes," he went on. "It seems—*is*—dreadful, if you like. But darling, I mean that you have everything ahead of you. At your age, this isn't a—matter of life and death."

She thought that it would, in fact, be easier to die than to get used to being without him. (But that, perhaps, was not a fair way of putting it, since it is really easier to die than to do almost anything.) The possibility of taking her own life was, however, something to be held in reserve, like a pain-relieving drug that can only be resorted to in extremity. It interested her to think that her words and actions would then assume an authority they could never command so long as there remained the possibility of

57

their repetition; it seemed hard that one should have to go to such lengths to make one's point.

If, on the other hand—as he suggested—she was merely beginning a series of similar experiences, she could scarcely feel encouraged. She sensed that she would never learn to approach love in any way that was materially different, or have the energy to go in for more than a little halfhearted dissembling. Up to this, she had led a life sheltered not from rancor and mistrust but from intimacy; nothing could convince her that this first sharing of her secret existence, more significant even than the offering of her person, represented less than it appeared to. That circumstances might oblige him to withdraw from her she perfectly understood; that he actually felt himself to be less committed appalled her. It confounded all her assumptions, that something so deeply attested should prove totally unpredictable.

She remembered her uncombed hair. Startling him, she got up quickly from the sofa and went into the bedroom. She stood at the dressing table, releasing her hair from the knot of ribbon, and then, with her hand on the hairbrush, stared into the mirror. After a moment, forgetting what she had come for, she sat down on the side of her unmade bed, propped one elbow sidewise on the pillows, and leaned her jaw on her hand.

When he appeared in the doorway, she made a small explanatory gesture with the hairbrush, which still dangled from her right hand, then reached across and replaced it on the dressing table. He leaned for a moment against the doorframe, and when he came into the room she curled her legs up on the crumpled sheets and drew back on the pillows, allowing him to sit at the foot of the bed. They passed, in this way, some minutes of that hot afternoon. Both had the sensation of leaving behind them, simply by changing the scene, the antagonism in the living room.

At last he reached out and took her hand again, as though needing for a little longer to be in touch with her. He frowned into space, and only turned his head when she spoke.

"Tell me," she asked him, in a voice that was now shaken and fatigued, "what we are going to do."

The hand holding hers opened briefly and closed again. "There aren't many possibilities. . . . We shall see less of each other. Not meet at all, perhaps." Incongruously, he added: "I will hate that."

After a pause she repeated, as if he had not answered her: "Tell me what to do."

He lowered his troubled, abstracted look to her head. "You could go abroad for a while," he said. "That might help."

They looked at each other. Her hand grasped his convulsively. "Tell me," she insisted, almost whispering, "something that won't be hard, or lonely."

"My dear," he said. Even to him, it was inconceivable that her love should not be reciprocated. In compassion, he kneaded her fingers for a moment with his own. "What

59

should I tell you? How happy I've been with you? How
many things you've done for me? That, in a way, you've
brought me back to life?" He let her hand go so that she
could lie back on the pillows, and stretched himself ex-
haustedly along the foot of the bed with one arm beneath
his head. Staring at the ceiling, he said: "I owe you everything."

This admission seemed to her to set the seal on the dis-
solution of their love: total indebtedness could only be
acknowledged where no attempt at repayment was contemplated. She closed her eyes on some sustained crest of
pain. Tears of desolation moved haltingly from the corners of her eyelids and disappeared into the hair above her
ears. She was scarcely aware of shedding these tears, drawn
as they were from weakness and the accessible surface of
grief; no such ready means of human expression could
give the real nature of sadness.

"I think I should go home," he said listlessly.

"Why?"

"We're just exhausting ourselves, like this. . . . Let's
hope we can see things more clearly tomorrow."

She gave a small regretful smile, her eyes still shut. 'I
think I must hope to see them less clearly." She felt him
sit up and lower his feet to the floor. She opened her eyes
as he rose and came round the bed to stand beside her.

"If I leave," he said, "you might get some sleep."

"Stay a minute," she said, still with that faint smile. She
put her hand up to the now creased edge of his jacket.

"I'm going to be so unhappy when you go, and I want to postpone it."

He sat down again, on the edge of the bed. Ineptly, he smoothed back her hair, and then drew his finger along the wet mark between her eye and ear. With an air of helpless simplicity, he said to her: "I'm sorry."

"My love," she said, in the same hushed voice. "It hurts me so."

"I know, I know." His fingers passed irresolutely down her head and began to spread out the tangled hair on her shoulder. "I know," he said again, half to himself. "It isn't easy."

He looked at her with such bewilderment that she raised her hand and laid it for a moment on his shoulder before letting it fall, hopelessly, across her body. After that she lay perfectly still, with her eyes on his face. This submissiveness and the slow familiar movements of his hand only served to emphasize the constraint of their attitudes. Neither of them spoke; the stillness in the room was the passionless, critical silence of a sickroom. He lifted her hand aside and unfastened the belt of her dress as gently and carefully as if she had had a serious accident, and he was ministering to her.

VITTORIO

VITTORIO stopped at Nannini's on his way home, and bought a cake. It was almost four o'clock, and the town was coming to life again after the siesta. The shop was already full of people; it was divided into a café and a confectioner's, and as he pondered the display of cakes Vittorio could hear behind him the clatter of cups and glasses at the bar, and the exchange of voices.

Leaning on the glass counter and waiting to be served, he began to feel foolish about the whole thing. He did not want a strange couple in his house. The idea would never have occurred to him had it not been for Francesco, his lawyer. It seemed to Vittorio than Francesco was interfering too much in his financial affairs. It was Francesco's suggestion that he should let rooms for the summer, and it was Francesco who had found the English couple who might at this moment, Vittorio thought anxiously, be arriving at his house to be interviewed. He rapped on the counter, and when the girl came selected a green cake with a pattern of crystalized fruits. As he waited for it to be wrapped, he pulled out of his pocket for the third time the piece of paper Francesco had given him, and stared at the name: Jonathan Murray.

Holding the red and gold cakebox by its loop of string, he made his way out of the shop. The girl at the counter and the girl at the *cassa* smiled at him; so did the policeman, as he crossed the main street: *"Buona sera, Professore."* The cake, he knew, had been observed and its purpose noted. The town, which had known what to expect of him for almost sixty years, could with a little application account for his slightest deviation from habit.

The house stood nearby, at the end of a narrow street, and he never approached it without being conscious of its charm. It had once belonged to his family and was now converted into apartments. Built in the twilight of Siena's glory and not truly medieval, it was not listed with the splendid little palaces that are among the town's attractions. Still, it was an elegant building of weathered white stone, with four narrow rows of arched windows along a curved façade. The entrance, as he stepped in from the June sunshine of the street, felt cool and dim and smelled like a church. The elevator was out of commission again, according to a notice dangling on the bars of its little cage, and he set off slowly up the shallow steps.

Giuseppina was at the door before he could ring. She was wearing, he saw, her best black dress and a starched apron, and her gray hair had been carefully strained back into its bun. How ridiculous we are, he thought, handing her the cakebox. I shall tell them that I've reconsidered, that there are no rooms. He began to smile at his own panic, while Giuseppina, in a lowered voice, reproached him for his lateness. "*E già venuta, la signora,*" she whispered, letting him pass.

He stopped at the hall mirror to straighten his tie. "*Ah, sì? E com'è?*"

She hovered beside him, the cakebox in both plump hands. "*Carina. Carina e gentile. Sta nello studio.*"

He ordered tea and went along the corridor to his study. The door was not quite closed, and as he pushed it open the afternoon light reached from the windows and made him pause. The woman who sat by his desk looked round and started to rise. He crossed the room quickly, murmuring in English: "Do sit down, how do you do," and she, taking his hand, replied: "I am Isabel Murray."

When she was reseated, Vittorio turned to adjust one of the shutters, deflecting the light from their faces. His first thought, as he drew up another chair, was that the room was shabby and hopelessly cluttered. His Persian rug, which he had always considered beautiful, was, he now saw, almost worn through; the leather arms of the chairs were white with use. Books had overflowed from the shelves onto the table and the desk, were even stacked on the floor. Among the ornaments on the piano, the photograph of his wife, Teresa, was warped and faded in its plush frame. The piano itself, which had scarcely been used since Teresa's death, was an antiquated upright of no distinction whatever, decorated with brass fittings for candles. He stared vaguely about as though he, rather than his visitor, were the prospective tenant.

His second thought, also accompanied by a sense of irritation, was that Mrs. Murray, as Giuseppina had suggested, was quite beautiful. Her face was almost a countenance—a pensive sunburned oval elaborated with brown eyes, a short nose, and a defenseless smile. Her fair hair, streaked by the sun, was coiled around her head and drawn to one side, in the style that was being worn in Italy that year—it was 1957. Her cotton dress was printed with blue flowers. About twenty-five or six, he supposed, looking at her almost with indignation, as though she had brought some disturbance into his house. She answered his look with her unsuspecting smile.

"My husband sends his apologies," she was saying. "He had to go to Florence for the day, on business."

"He is writing a guidebook?" asked Vittorio, wondering whether Francesco had got it right.

Apparently not, for Mrs. Murray hesitated, wrinkled her brow, and then said: "Well, a sort of guidebook. A description of the paintings, actually, in Siena. He went to Florence to see about reproductions. We expect to be here about two months, but it depends how long it all takes." She paused, and when he said nothing went on: "I believe you lived in England?"

65

"For nine years," he replied, thinking how remote his exile seemed to him. "I went there in 1937, after my wife's death, and came back in '46."

"I hope they were nice to you."

He smiled. "To be there at all, an Italian during the war, meant that I suffered. They realized that, and allowed me the stature of my condition. I have never known people so polite. And in my profession—I am a classicist—I could find immediately those who shared by interests."

"Well, I'm glad," she said, as though the responsibility had been her own.

"In England, life is a long process of composing one-self," he continued. "For us, the English are as strange as Orientals, with their formalities, their conventions, their silences. I should never have known, had I not lived there, how vulnerable they can be, and how sentimental."

On a tinkle of plates and silver, Giuseppina entered, bearing the tea tray. Vittorio, who took his tea each after-noon from a chipped ceramic mug, hastily cleared a space. The cake, ostentatiously intact, had been placed on a silver platter.

He began to spread the cups and saucers. "Or would you prefer a glass of something—*vin santo* . . .?"

"No," she said, "this is lovely. Shall I cut the cake?"

When they were established across the cups and plates, he asked: "Your husband—is he an artist himself?"

"No. He's doing a series of these books—last year we went to Perugia. It's just that he's interested in it. As a matter of fact, at Oxford he read classics," she added, not urging this bond. A little wedge of cake, crumbling between her fingers, fell to the floor, and she bent to pick up the pieces. "Your lovely rug," she said.

"Do you work, too?" he asked.

"Not very much, I'm afraid. I keep card indexes, and that sort of thing, and I go round with Jonathan, though sometimes he prefers to be alone. We've hired a Seicento, and we usually drive somewhere in the mornings—the book is on Siena and the surroundings. Yesterday we went to Rosia; the church there has a painting by . . ." She paused.

"Matteo di Giovanni," he supplied, pleased by her ignorance. In England, he had taught Latin at a girls' school for a short time, and he sketched to himself her education—a little implausible history, some disproportionate geography, and a muddled, lasting familiarity with the poets. The Latin, he knew through his own defeat, he could discount completely. He saw again rows of pale, virtuous faces inclined over blotched books.

There was a short silence. Vittorio put down his cup. "I should tell you about the house," he said, "or, rather, show it to you. You would have the bedroom and the *salotto*. The bathroom is next to the bedroom. I would, you see, move in here, into this room, so you wouldn't be disturbed. No, really," he said as her look deepened to protest, "I'd be much happier. I often sleep in here, when my brother comes from Rome. Unfortunately, being immediately under the roof, the apartment is quite warm in summer, but my father—the whole house was once his own—kept the top floor because of the view. What else? Well, there is hot water, but in the mornings only, I'm afraid." He hesitated again, and then mentioned uncertainly the price he had proposed to ask.

"It seems so little," she said.

"I thought it was too much," he answered, matching her ineptitude.

Jonathan Murray was so tall that he stooped to enter Vittorio's apartment, and so thin that sinews and veins were plainly seen on his taut, bare arm, which was weighted with a suitcase. He was in his middle thirties, a handsome, deliberate man with somber eyes and straight brown hair. Depositing the suitcase in the entrance hall, he turned to shake hands with Vittorio. His look, as far as courtesy would allow, held all things in abeyance, and it was Isabel, coming in behind him with a rug and a portable typewriter, who spoke first.

"The hotel wanted our room before lunch—I hope we're not too early. . . ." She let Vittorio take the typewriter. "Thank you. This is Jonathan."

Vittorio, silent and shy, led them along the corridor to where Giuseppina was making final adjustments to the bedroom. It was a large, lofty room, with walls of a spent green. The domed ceiling was white, and in one or two places flaking. The furniture, so heavily rooted as to appear a natural out-cropping of the floor, was of dark wood, and the bed was so wide it was almost square. The coverlet was the same faded gold as the central square of carpet, which lay on a floor of worn red tiles. On one wall, over a bookcase, were two framed photographs of Greek heads, and above the bed hung a worn reproduction on wood of a painting by Ambrogio Lorenzetti. The dark-green shutters were half closed against the morning sun; in the opening between them, at each of the two windows, was suspended a strip of Tuscan countryside.

The four of them stood in the middle of the room, like early guests at a party, trying to gauge affinities. Jonathan took the typewriter from Vittorio and put it on the floor by the bed.

"I hope you'll be comfortable," Vittorio said. "If you need anything, you will let me know?"

There was a murmur of thanks. Giuseppina, excused by the incomprehensible language, preceded him from the room.

Vittorio returned to his study and closed the door. He sat down at the desk, clasping his hands idly on the papers fanned out over the blotter, and waited for a feeling of imposition to overtake him. Apart from the occasional visits of his elder brother, Giacomo, who came from Rome on business connected with family property near Siena, he had not shared his house since Teresa's death. In England, the privacy of his lodgings in the house of a retired Indian Army major had been scrupulously respected; the major, indeed, had relaxed this principle on only one occasion, when he crossed Vittorio's threshold to press upon him a jar of hoarded chutney in celebration of the victory at El Alamein. Upon his return to Siena, Vittorio had entered the ordered seclusion of a celibate scholar. The greater part of each day was spent on his work—a third volume on aspects of classical Greek—and in the evenings he read. His social life was conducted almost exclusively in the café, where he could in the course of an hour or two meet everyone in the town whom he might wish to see. His friends were of his own condition—men of cultivated minds, distinguished manners, and diminished circumstances. The possibility of worldly success had never, by them, been entertained; they conjectured only as to the form their failure would take.

Three years earlier, Vittorio had bought a second-hand Topolino, and this extended his activities. From time to time, he drove into the hills to the south of Siena to inspect his family's villa, the house where he had spent his childhood and youth; closed and empty since the war, it was now the property of his brother Giacomo.

Vittorio was fifty-nine. He had considered and spoken of himself as an old man for so many years that his sixtieth birthday seemed long past, and he found it strange that he had yet to attain it. He dated his old age from the death of his wife twenty years before. Had it not been disloyal to Teresa, he would have admitted to himself that the date might be set even earlier; he could scarcely recall ever having felt sensations that might pass for youth. A

childhood burden of family disturbances had, by his early
marriage, been exchanged for the sorrow of Teresa's long
illness, and subsequently for the lonely anxiety of his exile.
His manner of living since his return to Siena represented
the first true peace he had experienced; he could not will-
ingly envisage any conclusion to it other than decrepitude
and death.

Because he recognized these things in himself, it surprised him to find that the arrival of the Murrays, caused
him, as yet, no pain. Distantly, through the closed door,
he could hear sounds of luggage pushed along tiled
floors, and the raised voice of Giuseppina; and once, into
a silence, flickered Mrs. Murray's laugh. He took up his
pen and lowered his hand to the page, but still did not
write, so greatly was he surprised by his own pleasure and
by an agreeable echo of what he presumed must be excite-
ment.

The spring that year was cool and wet, terminating in
a week of blinding heat that announced the summer.
Tourists wandered in the city's curving, shadowed streets
and climbed its narrow towers, and ultimately slumped
into chairs in the piazza, demanding iced drinks. Jonathan
Murray complained that his work in the museum was
interrupted by the monologues of German students and
the reluctant tramp of busloads of visitors. Isabel smiled
and, walking about the town, grew browner and seemed at
ease.

In the mornings, as she had told Vittorio, she and Jonathan usually drove out of the city to visit some nearby church or museum. Giuseppina took coffee to their room at an early hour, and before long Isabel would return the tray and its emptied dishes to the kitchen. Sometimes Vittorio was there discussing the day's housekeeping when she came in, dressed in her white robe, and stately because of the burden of the tray, her hair hanging down her back in a heavy plait that was frayed and flat from sleep. Leaning with both hands on the kitchen table and laughing at her own halting Italian, she would chat with Giuseppina, and Vittorio, watching her, wondered why all women didn't wear long hair.

When they returned after lunch, Jonathan went to the museum and Isabel rested through the early afternoon. At four o'clock, she took tea with Vittorio, although the ceremony of the cake was never repeated. He had thought his long, solitary afternoon essential and immutable, and was almost shocked to discover that a new habit could be so quickly, faithlessly formed. He found himself preparing for her with little imagined conversations that never came to birth, and afterward he wondered what they had talked about. Her presence seemed an immoderate, contrasting luxury in his room. As on the first day, she sat across from him, the shuttered light striping her hair and her burnished arm and distorting the colored pattern of her dress.

If Jonathan returned from the museum in time, he walked with Isabel to the piazza in the evening, but more often she went alone and waited for him in the café. Like other tourists, they read foreign papers in the fading light, and watched the crowd, and lived vicariously the pleasant life of the town. Jonathan inclined his head to Isabel's talk with a detached, indulgent smile, and sometimes Isabel, too, fell silent. Every evening, they dined out in Siena, and when they left the piazza in search of a *trattoria* they walked away with slow, grave purpose, like members of a procession.

If they were still in the café when Vittorio arrived before dinner for his ritual Campari, he sat with them until it was dark, or when he was with friends stopped at their table to exchange greetings. He found Jonathan rather solemn for an Englishman, and almost defensively earnest about his work. His knowledge, which was considerable, seemed sheltered within reticence, as though it were too precious to be made a source of general pleasure. Vittorio wondered whether life were ever difficult for Isabel. He understood that they had been married for four years.

One evening, he did not find them when he arrived at the café, although a mild, beautiful day had brought him there earlier than usual. The café was on a slight elevation commanding the paved shell of the piazza, and he looked about with a tender, habitual pleasure at the ripe rose and gold of the buildings and the soaring rocket of the campanile. The open space fluttered with bright dresses and blue shirts and indolent pigeons. One or two passers-by raised their hands to him in greeting, and the waiter, approaching the table with a tray under his arm, made him a little bow and wished him good evening.

"*Buona sera, Sergio,*" returned Vittorio. "*Come va?*"

"*Eh, Professore, si tira avanti; si tira avanti.*"

They contemplated the view for a moment together before Sergio disappeared to fetch Vittorio's Campari. Vittorio put on his reading glasses and took up his newspaper. As he did so, he thought he saw Isabel coming toward him across the square, and he paused, the folded paper in one hand. He could not be sure that it was she, and as she drew near he removed his glasses, crinkling his eyes into the late sunshine. When she was still some paces away, he stared at her and said, quite loudly: "You've cut your hair!"

She sat down beside him and laid her parcels on the table. Her hair, which exuded a singed, scented smell, framed her face in two Ionic curves just above her shoulders. She balanced one foot on the rod beneath the table.

Vittorio placed his paper and glasses on the cloth before him. "But why?"

She made a small, incompetent gesture. "Well, you know. It gets hot in summer, and when you wash it, it takes so long to dry. And then—Jonathan complained that there were long hairs over everything. . . ." She touched her head curiously. "I expect it will grow again."

"How long did it take to grow before?"

"Six years." She looked grave for a moment, and then began to laugh, partly at his agitation.

The waiter came up with Vittorio's Campari and looked at her mournfully. "*Si è tagliata i capelli, la signora.*"

Vittorio, glancing at her lowered, reddened face, gave Sergio a commiserating nod and, taking up his paper once more, ordered for her.

"I didn't think there would be such a fuss," she said.

He smiled. "The whole town will know by tomorrow."

"Hello," said Jonathan, making his way among the tables. He sat down on the other side of Isabel. "I got the *Observer*—I thought you might have bought the *Times* already. Have you ordered yet?" He looked around for Sergio. "You've had your hair cut."

"What do you think?" she asked, again raising her hand to her head.

"I suppose it's more practical." He leaned back in his chair, surveying the square.

Vittorio, absorbed in his own newspaper, avoided Sergio's eyes.

Jonathan spent the following morning at Asciano. Isabel stayed behind, promising to complete his card index, but she soon left the unsorted cards on the *salotto* table and went out shopping. She had lunch in the town, and Jonathan, returning earlier than expected, missed her and went to lunch alone. In the afternoon, he went back to the house on his way from the cathedral to the museum, and was told by Giuseppina that Isabel had come in some time ago and was having tea with Vittorio.

That evening, he left the museum before it closed and went straight home. He entered their room quietly, and closed the door behind him.

She was sitting at the mirror, painting her nails. She smiled into his reflection, but when he bent to kiss her she cried out: "Oh, be careful—my nails!"

He turned away impatiently and sat down on the bed, his hands on his knees.

She got up and came to him. He moved his feet apart to let her come between his knees, not lifting his hands. She rested her wrists on his shoulders, the fingers stiffly extended to dry.

"For God's sake, stop thinking about your nails. I've been looking for you all day." He looked up at her crossly. "Do you love me? An absurd question, as you're hardly likely to say no, even if you wanted to."

"It could be important that I went on *pretending,* couldn't it?" she asked. "That might be a kind of love." She frowned. "I don't much care for this conversation, though; couldn't we have a shot at something else?"

"The thing is," he went on, "that I need you. You know that, I suppose?"

"And you resent it."

"Yes," he said, "of course. But it could be worse, couldn't it? I mean, I don't shout at you or anything."

"You have no reason to."

"There wouldn't have to be a reason," he explained, reasonably. "What would you do if I did?"

"Cut my throat, perhaps?" she suggested.

He lowered his head against her arm. "That would ruin my whole life."

"And mine, too, presumably." She leaned against him. "Jonathan."

"Yes."

"Did anyone ever call you Jon?"

He thought. "In the Army they called me Jon. I rather liked that. It made the whole thing seem more unreal than ever."

"It's funny to think of you in the war. Being brave and everything."

"It helps," he responded dryly, "if you remember how much younger I was."

She half smiled. "You know what I mean. Explosions and death, and so on. It all seems too . . . immediate, for you."

"You should have married someone—immediate, as you say." He was silent for a moment. "I was thinking that yesterday, in the piazza. You know, when I showed up and everyone was dying for me to make a scene about your hair?"

"I understood about that," she said.

"Well, perhaps that's your trouble; you understand too readily. It makes it so easy for me. Anyway, I thought, Yes, that's what she needs. Someone who *would* make a scene. Someone who would make her his life's work. Someone like old Vittorio."

"What do you mean?" she said, not moving.

"What I mean, darling, is that the poor old chap's head over heels in love with you—in his quaint, Old World way, I hasten to add." He raised his head. "Did you realize that?"

"Well, yes, I did," she replied, "of course."

He shut his eyes. "That's what I can't bear about women. They always know everything first. They behave as though men were—Americans in Europe." He looked at her again. "Well, don't look like that. I'm not suggesting it's reciprocated. Hardly. It's just that he'd really be so much better for you, *mutatis mutandis*."

She drew away from him, clasping her hands vaguely against her breast, her nails forgotten. "What did you do today?" she asked.

"I went to Asciano, to see the museum at the church," he said. "And I saw a Sassetta in a private collection."

"Was it nice?" she inquired politely.

He smiled. "Well . . . it was a Sassetta."

She went back to her chair and took up the little bottle of lacquer. Jonathan watched in the mirror the uneven strokes of her hand and the sealed calm of her brow. He raised his head to speak again, but did not, although Isabel's hand paused at the abrupt intake of his breath. Presently he lay back across the bed and closed his eyes.

One hot afternoon at the end of July, Vittorio was returning from his brother's empty villa. He usually inspected the house every three or four weeks, sending

78

Giacomo a note about anything that had to be done. The responsibility was something of a burden to him, for his visits left him dispirited, less by the nostalgia they evoked than by its insufficiency. He had always been resigned to the course of his life.

Driving into the city, he was obliged to circle the large piazza at the post office, and as he slowed at its central plot of garden he saw Isabel at a café table, reading in a patch of shade.

He drew the car up under a red and blue umbrella marked "Punt e Mes." "Mrs. Murray!" he called. "Mrs. Murray!" She did not hear him. He turned off the engine and, getting out of the car, went up to her table.

She was so startled that she splashed coffee into the saucer as she set down her cup. She looked up, shading her eyes and pointing with her other hand to the chair beside her.

He shook his head. "I've left the car over there, in the street. I've been to my brother's house. I wondered if you'd like a lift home."

"It would be nice," she said, as if she meant to refuse. But she rose and took up her handbag and book. Vittorio called the waiter.

Opening the car door, he cleared away a week-old copy of La Stampa and helped her in. They left the shadow provided by "Punt e Mes" and moved patiently into the main street, which was choked with its afternoon tide of cars and scooters and incautious pedestrians.

"Was it a long drive to your brother's house?" she asked.

79

"It only takes about twenty minutes by the Grosseto road," he told her. "When I was a boy, of course, we were much more isolated. It was considered a real journey to Siena. People didn't drop in—if they came at all, they stayed. And then, my father, as he got older, was more and more withdrawn from the world."

"What did he do?"

"He was a classical scholar—a good one." He smiled, not quite painlessly. "My name is the same as his, and I am always asked if I wrote his books. Giacomo—there were only the two of us—became an archaeologist, but it was understood that I should be a classicist; just as some families put one son into the Church. Though, as it happened, it was what I would have chosen." How boring this must be, he thought, especially to the English, who don't discuss themselves in this way. They had come to a standstill in the traffic, and, turning to confirm his dullness in her expression, he found her watching him, instead, with gentle concern. He smiled at her and added: "So you see, it didn't matter after all." He scarcely knew himself what he intended by the remark, except that all the obscure concessions of his life seemed with a deliberate, perverse extravagance to have brought him into her company.

They moved forward and were halted again, a little farther on, by a traffic light. "You will be leaving soon," he said, with the air of making an announcement.

"Early next month," she replied.

"That is sad."

After a moment, she said: "Perhaps we'll come to Italy again next year."

"I meant, for me." She doesn't know, he decided.

"Yes, I know," she said.

He thought, because at that moment he felt he could bear it, of how they would go away in a week or two; they would write him, together, one nice letter and perhaps a few post cards. The light changed to green, and he turned the corner into his own short street.

When he had parked the car, Isabel closed her window. Vittorio turned off the engine and, waiting for her to gather her things together, pulled his glasses out of his pocket and took up her book to examine its title. It was one of his own works.

He could not have been more embarrassed had he found her praying. "*Accidenti!*" he said. "How dull for you. But do you—?"

"Understand anything? Well, no, not much, naturally."

"Then why ever do you bother?"

Isabel took the book back and started to get out of the car. She looked oppressed and, he thought at first, offended. He opened his own door and went round to hers, astonishment still in his face.

And it was with astonishment, more than anything else, that he saw her eyes enlarge with tears before she turned from him toward the house—an unbearable astonishment that called upon all his capacities for comprehension. He followed her in silence. They entered the house together and began to climb the stairs. He was profoundly aware of her, moving slowly and sadly at his side, but it did not occur to him to speak. He felt that he must be alone to think about it, that there must be some rational, disappointing explanation. He could scarcely breathe, from the stairs and from astonishment. He had never been so astonished in his life.

IN ONE'S OWN HOUSE

"I HOPE we didn't wake you, Miranda," Constance said.

Miranda had come downstairs in her dressing gown, forgetting that her mother-in-law always appeared at breakfast fully dressed. And there she was, Constance, in a linen dress and a green sweater, pouring out coffee. This early rising and dressing on Constance's part was rather uncharacteristic. She herself readily explained it to her guests as the necessity of setting a good example. "In one's own house," she would then add—it was an expression she was particularly fond of.

In other respects, Constance affected a charming disorder, which turned to downright vagueness in the face of other people's difficulties. Of independent mind and means ("a widow with a little money" was another of her favored phrases), she repudiated, shrewdly or selfishly, untidy elements in the lives of others. Within her own controlled variety of moods, coy or unfeeling, she maintained a handsome serenity—like a country that, suffering no extremes of climate, remains always green. Her affection was largely reserved for her younger son, James, now seated beside her at the breakfast table, holding his coffee cup in both his hands and resting his elbows on the edge of the table. With her other son, Miranda's husband Russell, she had never felt at ease. She saw him seldom—when he and Miranda visited her here in the country, or on her own rare trips to New York. She thought him sarcastic, intense, unknowable; his attitude toward her seemed to be one of continual reproach, and she could not help wondering what, in his mind, he accused her of. She was distressed, but not surprised, that he had managed to have a nervous breakdown.

Miranda said: "Oh no, not at all," and seated herself opposite James. At the other end of the table, a fourth place had been laid for Russell.

"Of course, time *is* getting on," Constance continued, "if you want to go to church."

"*Church?*" inquired James.

"Miranda does go to church," Constance rebuked him, the soul of open-mindedness.

"I went once," Miranda told him, "when we were here at Easter. I was the only woman without a hat. I felt like the Infidel."

"I'm sure, my dear, you get credit for good thoughts." Constance took Miranda's cup. "Like Abou ben Adhem," she added kindly.

"The sermon was very dull," Miranda said, placatingly.

84

"I don't doubt it." Having filled the cup, Constance passed it back. "I always think, don't you, that Catholic churches must be much more interesting than ours. So much more going *on*. Protestants are so docile—turning up in pairs on Sunday, like animals entering the Ark." After an insufficient pause, Constance went on: "Well, Miranda dear, you must go to church just as often as you like—if you really do mean to spend the summer here."

Miranda, unresisting, drank her coffee.

"Isn't Russell coming to breakfast?" James helped himself to the last piece of toast without waiting for the answer to this question.

"He's still sleeping," Miranda said. "I'll take a tray up to him when we've finished."

Constance felt—and not for the first time—that Miranda was indulging Russell. Which may well be the cause of his trouble, she added to herself. Aloud, she pointed out that there was still hot coffee in the pot. "If you want to call him now," she suggested.

Miranda almost sighed. "No," she said. "I think he should sleep. He has a long journey ahead of him tomorrow."

"My dear, he gets on a plane in New York and gets off it in Athens. That isn't so strenuous, after all."

Miranda thought it sounded utterly exhausting, but said nothing.

James said to Miranda: "Are you going to New York with him?"

"No. I'll drive him to New Haven and see him off on the train."

"Why don't you go to New York?"

Miranda said bravely: "Because he doesn't want me to," and began to collect the empty dishes within her reach.

Damn Russell, thought James; everything connected with him led to trouble and hurt someone's feelings. Rather, hurt Miranda's feelings—and that's all I care about, he said to himself—looking at her briefly, so that his mother wouldn't notice, but seeing everything: her meekly attentive face, still faintly smeared with night cream and dominated by her wide, now colorless mouth, the straight black hair she had already brushed into a careful line along her shoulders, and the rose-colored dressing gown that opened on the white curve of her breast. Damn Russell, thought James.

Oh Russell, my darling, why must you do this, Miranda wondered, grieving above the plates and cups. Is it really going to help you to be away, to be without me? Will you really come back? She pushed her chair out from the table and wrapped her dressing gown about her, resting her hand for a moment against her body. It's strange, she thought, that these trite expressions should have such meaning—"My heart bleeds"; "It cut me to the heart"...
One *does* feel it here. Something to do, perhaps, with circulation or breathing.

"A very good color for you, Miranda, that pink," Constance declared. She had a proprietary way of admiring other people's possessions, as if all good taste were in some measure a tribute to herself. "Yes, an excellent color," she repeated, in this flat, confiscating manner of hers, as Miranda trailed out of the dining room toward the kitchen. Then she looked adoringly at James, who was still eating his breakfast.

Constance's husband had died in the war, shortly after James's birth. The fact that she had, unaided, raised this remarkable young man was a daily source of gratification to her. James's strong and subtle personality, his intelligence, his good looks would have more than met her own requirements. That he should, into the bargain, have turned out to be charming and kind was an unlooked-for bonus that, as far as Constance was concerned, simply vindicated his gifts in the eyes of a jealous society. He was so attractive, she sometimes thought, that he was really entitled to be a bit nasty; instead—magnanimously, she felt—he was very nice. He would go a long way—always in the right direction; they all said so, his professors, his college friends, even Russell. Russell himself had done well enough, until now, but James would do more. James was more singular, his talents less diffuse. If only, she prayed, if only he would get over these grotesque notions about Miranda. (Thank God Miranda herself hadn't noticed yet.) It really couldn't be worse, if the two of them were to be in the house all summer. "Poor little Miranda's looking rather drawn, I thought," she said.

"Seemed all right to me," James replied. "Perhaps she'll cheer up after Russell goes."

Someone will cheer up anyway, Constance thought

grimly, watching him. "She'd be better advised to cheer up beforehand. It only makes Russell worse to see her subdued like this."

"Russell's not exactly clamorous himself," James pointed out. He wiped his hands on a paper napkin and left it in a ball on his plate. "And never has been."

"All the more reason for Miranda to provide a little contrast. . . Proust, if you recall, says that Swann was instinctively repelled by the very women whose depth of character and melancholy expression exactly reflected his own."

"I don't, no."

"Don't what?"

"Recall." But James was pleased to note that his mother had inadvertently credited Miranda with a depth of character she usually managed to deny her.

Constance got up from the table, picked up James's empty dishes, and followed Miranda to the kitchen. She found her daughter-in-law leaning one elbow on top of the refrigerator, waiting for the toast to be done. A set tray stood on the kitchen table.

"May I take the paper for Russell?" Miranda asked.

"Oh of course. I'll see it later."

"Oh, not if you're not finished with it."

"My dear, I'm sure there's nothing of interest in it. I can very well wait." Constance watched Miranda buttering the toast. "Though I must say, Miranda, I don't think you ought to pander to Russell quite so much."

Why must you say it, Miranda wondered. "Constance,"

she said, carefully putting butter at the corners of the slice, "Russell is very sick."

Sick, Constance repeated to herself, now thoroughly exasperated. *Sick.* People seem quite incapable of using straightforward words these days. My son questions, as well he might, the very nature of our existence, and they discuss him as though he had German measles. Sick—that's the word they use now when people become exercised over the human condition. Sick, indeed. "Do you have any idea, Miranda darling, how all this started?"

Miranda put the toast on the tray and took the coffee off the stove. "It's a long story," she said.

When one says that it's always something fundamental that could be explained in a single sentence, Constance remarked to herself. She pushed the door open for Miranda to pass through.

Turning back into the room, she saw that Miranda had left the newspaper on the table.

When Russell had finished his breakfast he lay in bed with his hands folded under his head and watched Miranda making up her face. He could see that this unnerved her, from the attention with which she handled the succession of little jars.

"Why do you need all of those?"

"Oh, they're all different, you see."

"They can't *all* be different. It's ridiculous. An obsession."

She thought with mild resentment of the equipment he carried on his own person. He was always looking for his lighter, running out of cigarettes, forgetting his glasses. She, who did not smoke or wear glasses, would not have dreamed of complaining of these things. But his irritation, she knew, was not concerned with the jars on her dressing table: directed at herself, it was the antithesis of love.

"Oh—perhaps you're right. It's probably silly."

"I hate the way you keep saying 'Oh.' " He saw, in the mirror, her eyes deflect. "And the way you keep agreeing."

"Agreeing?"

"Humoring me. Backed like a weasel. Very like a whale. How true, my lord."

She lowered her head, defeated, and began to put the contents of the dressing-table drawer in order. These onslaughts of his were like outcroppings of rock in the surface of her day. Sometimes, as now, her heart twisted and broke under his determination to wound her. At others, she was almost convinced that she felt nothing more for him, that he had overdrawn on her endurance: then she would stay silent for a while, almost at peace, beyond his reach, not knowing whether she had been utterly vanquished or become completely invincible. However, it required merely some slight attention on his part to restore all her apprehensions—for these extremes of feeling only existed within the compass of her love.

Russell, still watching her, experienced the sensation of being abandoned that always accompanied such victories, as if he had lost the one person who connected him to reality, whose very pain was a guiding thread in the endless labyrinth of his anguish. He thought with despair of her selfishness, all her anxiety for him originating in her own need for his love. She imagines, he thought bitterly, that I could simply be *nicer* to her; that I could easily be kind if I wanted to, treat her better if I would only try. She had completely failed to realize how far he had descended into this dark place from which no consoling speech could deliver him, no outstretched hand—even hers—bring him back. While *she*, at one word from him, could be fully restored to life and power and thought. What could she complain of, then, he demanded of her inclined head. Her misery was vicarious, almost parasitical; she knew its cause precisely. It might, in fact, be said of her that she stood continually at the brink of utter happiness. Why, she should count herself among the most fortunate of mortals—blessed art thou among women, Miranda Richmond.

But occasionally he did feel her suffering—as it were, through the screen of his own. The night before, they had lain down in silence, immensely remote from each other in this comfortable bed in his mother's best guest room. He had behaved so cruelly to Miranda all day that he knew he could not decently approach her (here he made a mental note to be more careful this evening), and they slept without touching. But that morning he had wakened very early and watched her sleeping—her grief showing even then, for her closed fist was pressed against her mouth as if she had fallen asleep stifling her sobs. For a moment he had wanted intensely to awaken and reassure her, to take her out of sleep back into his embrace before she could recollect what stood between them. For that moment he had lain wanting her to know that help was at hand. But the moment passed, and with it the impulse to rescue her. He could not face her surprise, her pleasure, her tears. He could not face his own inability to sustain this moment of sanity, and the absolute certainly of her disappointment.

"I must say these things, you know," he told her, in a fairly pleasant voice. "I don't care for them either, but they do come out, ugly as they are."

She turned round on the stool and looked at him. "Russell, tell me why."

He lowered his eyes from the ceiling and looked at her again, still with his hands behind his head. "I suppose they represent me at the moment—I mean, that I *am* ugly. Wouldn't you think? Something like that?"

"No."

"I tell you yes, Miranda. That's the way it is. Envy-and-calumny-and-hate-and-pain, darling—the bloody lot." He smiled at her. "Where's the paper?"

"I didn't bring it up. I think Constance wanted to see it."

"Oh, *she's* turned nasty again, has she? God, darling, I can't see you sticking out the summer here. Even the city in a heat wave is better than Constance."

"She's not so bad. You have to know how to handle her."

"Which, as it happens, neither of us does."

Miranda laughed. She took off her rose-colored gown and started to dress.

"Could you hand me those folders." He sat up and took a bundle of travel leaflets from her. She sat on the bed at a little distance from him, buttoning her dress. Between them, over the blanket, he spread a topographical map of the Greek peninsula and the islands. "You understand that I have to do this?" he asked her, for the twentieth time. "That I have to be away—be alone?"

For the twentieth time she responded: "Oh yes." She subdued the folds of the map with her fingers. She bent her head over the fantastic pattern of blue sea and green islands with an assiduous show of interest, like a child examining an invitation for a party to which she has not been asked.

"I may go to France later," Russell remarked unsparingly. The studied absorption of her attitude and his awareness of her unshed tears could not touch him. He felt again that she was obtruding her trivial, untimely demands on to a scene of disaster, and he felt justified in setting her down. Being away from all this, and from her, was now the only prospect that gave him pleasure; tomorrow could not come quickly enough. And yet—the idea of anyone else receiving this tender, faultless love of hers, or being subjected to its relentless self-denial, was unthinkable. Even if he never came back to her—though he supposed he would—he must be able to think that she wanted him, always. "Was James around this morning?" he asked, discarding one pamphlet after another.

"He was having breakfast," she said.

"Is he going to hang about here all summer? Really, Constance indulges him. I always had to work at least part of the vacation."

"She does spoil him, of course. It's the gap in your ages, don't you think?" Russell was fourteen years older than James. "Still, James is turning out rather well." Miranda cast about uneasily for a means of turning the conversation. She felt it would be the last straw if James's interest in her, ridiculous as it was, were to come to Russell's attention now.

Russell could only hope that James would get over it soon. It was better, he had decided, not to mention anything to Miranda. But she really was impossible—any other woman would have noticed such a thing immediately. She lives in a world of her own, he thought, as he looked at her innocently sorting the papers on the bed. "I suppose it's time I got up," he said.

"Where's Miranda?" James asked, when Russell appeared alone in the bright garden.

"She had letters to write." Russell walked on down the path, nodding to his mother, who sat, sewing buttons on a shirt, in a cane chair beside James. James's effrontery, the ineptitude of Miranda now ceased to interest him. He walked along the flagged path, onto which the flood tide of his mother's flowers had overflowed, fully engaged in maintaining his own equilibrium. This required an effort so intense that it became, at times, almost, physical and he walked like a person under a strong sedative, slightly stupefied, his body braced against the return of pain. In so far as he noticed at all, he saw only a threat in the brilliant delicacy of the flowers, the smooth sweep of grass, and the light shredded through trees and shrubs at the end of the path. These were things—unlike his relations with Miranda, or his inability to work, which were matters inextricably entangled with his life—offered gratuitously by fate to impede his struggle for sanity. He felt that if he did not soon reach a place of shelter and darkness he would have to turn and go back inside. He crossed the foot of the lawn and pushed his way into a small wood with the instinctive haste of someone who, at the point of suffocation, seeks fresh air.

"This seems to be one of Russell's bad days," remarked Constance, looked troubled.

"I can't make out what's wrong with him," James said.

"He's just dreadfully depressed, dear. He feels we're all doomed—which is, after all, no more than the truth, though one can't afford to give it undivided attention. These things happen to people—they say he will get over it. It's as though the Life Force has been temporarily cut off."

"You make it sound like part of the utilities. In the meantime, how awful for Miranda."

Constance's frown deepened. "Well, my dear, she must

take the rough with the smooth, as the marriage service says." After this somewhat loose quotation, she paused to examine the rest of the buttons on the shirt, and attacked one with her needle. "Marriage is like democracy—it doesn't really work, but it's all we've been able to come up with . . . Given the best of circumstances, it's exceedingly difficult. I suppose, if Dan had lived"—Dan was Constance's husband—"we would have had our difficulties too." Constance only said this to make her point: nothing would have made her believe, particularly in retrospect, that she and Daniel might ever have quarreled.

"What will Miranda do with herself while he's gone?"

"I've been wondering about that. Perhaps she might get out her things and do a little painting again. If we were nearer to a town, she might have taken a little job." All Miranda's accomplishments seemed to be diminutive ones. "If she had been more conclusively religious—and I must say she is just the type for it—it would have been a splendid opportunity to make a Retreat." She snipped a thread, and then added: "As though one ever makes anything else."

Miranda was writing to her mother. She had just put "Russell is very excited about his trip" (since this was another person whose abundant sorrows left no room for Miranda's), when the door opened. She looked up quickly, expecting her husband's haggard face to give her words the lie, but it was not Russell who came into the room.

"Oh, James," she murmured, her elbow on the table, her pen in the air. He might have knocked, she thought.

"I thought you might like the paper." He laid it on the bed and then sat down beside it. He crossed one foot over his knee and leaned forward, grasping his ankle.

She went on writing and, after a pause, said dismissingly: "Thank you."

He continued to sit there on the edge of her bed. He saw Russell's two suitcases, half-packed by Miranda, on the floor near the door; Russell's jacket over a chair; Russell's black leather slippers near his own feet. He looked about the room, repelled by all these implications of Russell's presence, all these reminders that Russell was privileged to enter at any moment—without knocking and without incurring Miranda's frown. It pained him to think that Russell and Miranda were so much together, so much alone; he was appalled by the idea that they made love.

He got up and wandered first to the windows, and then to the dressing table. This at least seemed to be entirely Miranda's. He picked up a bottle or two, and set them down with an unpracticed hand. "Is this your scent? . . . How fascinating—all these little jars." Miranda glanced up briefly but did not speak, and he sat down again on the bed. "Dearest Miranda," he said. "I would do anything to comfort you."

This time she did not look up. "Stop that," she said. She signed her letter, and took out an envelope and addressed it.

"Anything," he repeated.

"I don't need comforting," she told him. Unconsciously giving a more gentle echo to Russell's savage denunciations, she said: "I have nothing to complain of. It's Russell who needs to be comforted."

"What's the matter with him anyway?" James asked this in a tone of anticipatory disbelief, but Miranda looked up from a fresh page to give him a serious answer.

"He is in despair," she said. "Not the sort of despair that you or I might have, for a day or two, to be shifted by circumstances or surmounted by an effort of the will, but something that seems to him, I imagine, almost—like a discovery of the truth."

"But why, Miranda? What could be wrong with him? He has a good life." James, indeed, felt that Russell had cause for perpetual rejoicing.

"Young as you are," Miranda began heartlessly, "you must already know that the ebb of meaning in life is unaccountable. I'm sure Russell is going to get over this. But I saw it approaching for a long time. . . No, I can't tell you why. Some of it may be my fault." Because this was unbearable to her, she had to add: "Though they say not." She went back to her writing, and James allowed a decent interval before he reverted to what was for him the main topic.

"Do you know—you're more yourself with me than with anyone else. I mean, in talking, that kind of thing."

This was so irrefutably the case that after a moment she simply said "Yes."

"Why is that?"

"It must be," she said, "because you have nothing I want."

"That's cruel."

She thought that yes, she was being cruel. But it was the truth. She wanted Russell's love, Constance's approval, and her relations with each were pervaded with constraint and supplication. James's reactions were of practically no interest to her—or was it, she wondered, more complicated than that: that she knew he would, for the present at least, go on caring for her no matter what she said to him?

James continued: "I, on the other hand, am better with anyone else than with you."

"Goodness, why?"

"I suppose I can't think of anything good enough to say to you. Anything worthy of you. And then—you make me feel that I'm young."

Heavens, she thought, studying the paper before her. He thinks I am a woman of the world. She gave an inward smile of astonishment. "I'm ten years older than you." she said. "Ten important years."

He said suddenly: "Miranda, I love you so. . . Now what's the matter? Can't I even say the word?"

"It seems rather like taking the name of the Lord thy God in vain."

"In vain? What do you think this is, then, if not love?"

"Oh—something to do with the spring," she said lightly. "The regenerative process."

He said sullenly: "I'm not thinking of the regenerative process."

She smiled. "But it may be thinking of you."

"But I do love you. You *must* feel something."

"Why?" she asked coldly, addressing another envelope. "Why must I? I have been your age and in love—we all have. And had nothing from it."

"Then—what happens?"

"What happens?" she looked up, again with large serious eyes. "Why . . . it just hurts and hurts until it wears out." They stared at each other in dismay for a moment, and then she went on: "James, don't you feel any loyalty to Russell?"

"You mean, in connection with you? He treats you so badly."

"That isn't for you to say. I meant—because he's fond of you."

"Well, it *is* all rather biblical, I must say."

"It might be, if it were serious."

"But it *is* serious. Miranda, it *is*."

She leaned back a little in her chair. "James, don't be absurd. What could you possibly hope for from me?"

"It's what I wonder myself, of course—I see there isn't anything. . . I suppose I hope that you would like me a little, and show it—would say something I could remember and be pleased about. . . And then—these are my wildest imaginings—I think we might go away together for a while."

She kept calm. She said, with a faint smile: "Your mother would be displeased." (And with reason for once, she added to herself.)

"We could go away separately, and meet."

It would be frightful, she thought, imagining it all in the space of a second. Everyone in the hotels would see the difference in our ages. We would run into someone we know. I would have to pay—I would hate that. "That's enough. Now leave me alone," she said.

"Let me stay."

"No." She went on writing, annoyed at last.

"I shan't bother you. I promise."

Glancing at him, she saw that his face had altered and was full of pain. He unclasped his hand from his ankle and extended it a little toward her. "Let me stay," he said again. "You don't have to say anything to me. It's simply to see you. To know what you're doing. Be in the room with you." He stared at her, his hand opened in that artless appeal.

She stopped writing and, still holding the pen, rested her brow on her hand and shielded her eyes in what he took to be a gesture of exasperation. It was, instead, that she felt suddenly touched. To make oneself completely vulnerable, to offer one's love without reserve—even Miranda had long since lost that capacity, before she met and married Russell. You learned—it was all understood—that you must not forfeit any advantage, and that love itself was a subtle game of stoutly maintaining or judiciously

yielding your position. . . She was all at once ashamed of
this seedy knowledge, and envied his ability to declare
himself. From behind her arduously constructed defenses,
she felt she had now no way even to pay tribute to his
generosity, his innocence; to love itself. She sat still, with
her hand over her eyes.

"James? I think he must be studying," Constance said.

Russell removed James's book from the chair, dropped
it on the grass, and sat down. He looked sideways at his
mother, and then shifted his position so that he could see
the garden. Constance went on sewing, apparently unaware of his restlessness. Finally he lay back in the chair
and looked at the sky. After a moment, however, he turned
his head again, and said abruptly: "Be kind to Miranda
this summer." He felt a little awkward, delegating to his
mother the task he had been incapable of performing
himself.

"Well of course," replied Constance, too readily. "It's
why I suggested she come here. You know I'm devoted to
her."

You're a hard, frivolous woman, Russell thought. "You're
very kind," he said.

"Not at all. It was the least I could do."

And therefore you did it, he observed. "Miranda's un-
worldly," he said. "She has no idea of looking after herself."

If he's worried about James, Constance thought with

justifiable edginess, he should stay here himself; how could I possibly interfere in that? "Don't you worry," she told him. "We'll take care of her."

How can I leave Miranda to this, Russell wondered. He said: "I'll write as soon as I get there."

"Russell." Constance laid down her sewing and looked at him. "Is there anything I can do for you? If you aren't going to work for all these months, you may need some money."

Oh Christ, Russell thought, she's not going to take it into her head to behave well. His antagonism to his mother was too deeply rooted to allow her any act of disinterested kindness. He said aloofly: "Thank you, Mother. No."

"If I can give you anything," she went on, "you would only have to ask."

But you *would* have to ask, Russell noted remorselessly. He would not meet Constance's earnest look. Of all her expressions, it was the one with which he was least familiar. He preferred to think of her more usual aspects—arch, superficial, peremptory: those moods of his mother's which he now found all the more infuriating because he had, as a boy, so greatly admired them.

No less defeated than Miranda, Constance took up her sewing. "I hope you'll get what you want from this trip."

Russell, relenting, gave her a wry, intimate smile he could never have given Miranda. "The main thing seems to be to get away . . . since all the things I should face up to are here. I feel like a fugitive from justice."

Constance was herself again. She sighed. "We are all that," she said.

"Do you think you'll be able to get out of here?" Russell asked, having parked the car, miraculously, in a short space outside the station. He turned off the engine.

Miranda nodded. Reversing the car and driving home belonged to afterwards, when she would be alone. She would not think of that. How disproportionate, she marveled, were the varied limits of human endurance: she, who got sick if she sat in the sun, or fainted if she had to stand too long in a crowd, would survive this devastating morning without any appreciable loss of physical control and would, in fact, conclude it with a twenty-mile drive. She began to gather up Russell's papers from the floor of the car.

It will be better for her when I'm gone, Russell thought. He really meant, It will be better for me—because he could have no peace in the presence of Miranda's pain. Once out of sight, her suffering would quickly become bearable to him. He pictured her driving home, putting the car away, going up to their—her—room, and closing the door. His imagination refused the next scene, where she lay down on the bed and wept.

Holding his books and magazines in her lap, she looked up at him and then away. He touched her white cheek with his hand. He said, with what was at that moment total irrelevance: "You're so beautiful, Miranda."

Without turning to him, she opened the door of the car and got out. He came round to the curb and unloaded his luggage from the back seat.

"Give me those," he said. He took two books from her and stuffed them in the pockets of his raincoat, which he laid on top of the suitcases. Then he stood still, between the car and the steel mesh fence of the parking lot, looking at her.

"Better watch the time," Miranda said. She had not lifted her eyes.

"I have plenty of time." Now, as he put his arms around her, her anguish communicated itself to him at last. He could feel it pressing onto his breast as she leaned against him, weightless, submissive. For an instant he wondered, with genuine mystification, What have I done to her? Will she ever get over this? He released her a little, and passed his fingers over her eyes and mouth in a curious, sightless gesture. "Don't come to the train," he said.

"Let me." She drew away from him. When he bent to pick up his luggage, she brought a handkerchief out of her pocket and wiped her eyes. They walked into the station side by side.

A train was coming in, at another platform, slowly obliterating the further wasteland of tracks, shunted locomotives, and spiritless grasses. As soon as it stopped, businessmen jumped off, holding newspapers and brief cases. Hands and handkerchiefs waved from windows and doors. Old people were helped down by the conductor, and young people sprang into each other's arms. The entire train was emptied in a matter of moments. One or two couples greeted each other silently, with an abrupt kiss, and walked away, scarcely speaking, not holding hands.

How will it be when he returns, Miranda wondered, watching them from the other platform; how will we greet each other? Will we be silent too? And if we speak, what will we have to say?

VILLA ADRIANA

THEY got down from the bus in the middle of a straight, flat stretch of the Via Tiburtina. It was the midday bus from Rome, loaded with visiting relatives and returning farmers, and at the windows heads turned to watch the two foreigners descend to the country road. First, the man got down, his camera strap over his shoulder, his jacket over his arm, a book in his hand. The bus waited, quivering. He extended his free hand to the woman, who, slightly gathering her dress, negotiated the deep steps.

"*Vanno alla villa*" was exchanged around the bus.

The conductor called to the driver, the door clanged, and they were left behind in a cloud of dust.

Because this was the higher part of the plain across which they had come, they could see it stretching back in the direction of Rome—a dry, untidy shrubbery posted with olive trees and cypresses and a litter of small houses, rammed by the sun. Behind them, where the bus was already climbing the steep slope to Tivoli, the mountains were white, almost featureless in the heat, and scrabbled with vineyards and umbrella pines.

"VILLA ADRIANA," said the notice under which they turned off into a lane. Where it joined the main road, the lane was quite suburban. It was lined with raw, shuttered houses and with groups of oleanders that gave no shade and weighted the air with a sugary smell. But a little farther the countryside closed in, and the two of them wandered on in shadow, scarcely speaking, her hand through the crook of his free arm. In the middle of a wood, the trees gave way to a parking area. Crossing this open space between two empty tourist buses, they entered the gates of the villa.

"So you see," she said, as though they had been having a long conversation, "there wouldn't be much point." They rounded a corner and stopped in the avenue to look at the ruins of a small amphitheater.

"This is called the Greek Theater." He closed his book, and they walked on between two lines of magnificent cypresses.

"I'm sure you agree," she continued, with that off-handedness, he thought, so uncharacteristic of her, that she had developed in these last few days—like a parody of what she objected to in his own manner. As if to irritate him even further, she added, "on the whole," as they paused at the top of the avenue before one extremity of a colossal wall.

There was a restaurant to their right, among the trees. "Shall we have something now, or later?" he asked her.

"It's so hot," she said.

He put his book in his pocket, and they went into the café and stood at the bar. They boy took two wet glasses from the draining board and filled them with *aranciata*. In the garden at the back, a girl was clearing the deserted lunch tables. Her stiff, short skirt spread out around her and exposed the backs of her knees each time she bent over to collect another dish. She took, in her high-heeled sandals, such tiny, tapping steps that it seemed she would never complete the journey from one table to the next. Now and then she glanced at the boy in the bar, and whenever she looked up he was watching her.

"On the whole" indeed, the man thought angrily as they left the café and passed through a gap in the great wall into an open field of ruins. "I'm not quite sure what we're talking about," he told her, although nothing more had been said.

"Simply that it wouldn't work." She stood still to gaze at a sheet of water, a long, shallow pond in which a few lilies were trailing. "We would make one another unhappy —we do already—and it's as well that we found out in time. That's all. It's quite impossible."

"I don't understand," he said stubbornly.

"And that," she returned, "is precisely why."

I must have hurt her vanity, he decided, since she was not usually cruel. Opinionated, sulky sometimes—but even that she couldn't sustain; she would give in at the first appeal. (Preferring consistency, he could not value such concessions.) If he were to say now, for example, whatever it might be she wanted him to say—that nothing mattered to him but their love for each other, something along those lines—she would come round. Though why she should need that, why she minded so, he couldn't imagine. She herself, after all, had other things in her life, had, in fact, loved before this, more intensely; he didn't know who it was—and had not the least desire to know, he told himself, his mind ranging hastily over the circle of their friends.

"I don't really think you care deeply about anything," she was saying now, as though the observation might be of passing interest. "Except, of course, your work."

He reflected that she was probably the only person he knew who didn't attach importance to his work. And it *was* important; something would be changed in the field, however imperceptibly, when his book came out. She, who knew nothing, nothing at all, and was always exalting her miserable intuitions into the sphere of knowledge—how dare she speak of his interest in his work as though it were something pedestrian, discreditable? She had no feeling for the elements, the composition of things. Once, for instance, in Rome, they had seen an ancient inscription on a wall, and he had begun to translate it aloud when she, brushing aside the syntax, rendered the sense of it in half a dozen words and turned away, having temporarily deprived him of his reason for living.

"Perhaps it's true that I care most about my work," he said. "But then I do care—about other things. In any case, I can't be what I'm not."

They were walking now on a path of small stones.

She persisted, relentlessly: "You gave a different impression when we first knew each other."

He halted, opening his hands helplessly. "Well—that was human."

This, unexpectedly, seemed to be an acceptable answer, and they turned off the path into a vast shell of red Roman brick, and entered an inner courtyard. Water was seeping over the ruined paving and around the plinths of the broken columns that unevenly supported the sky. Releasing his arm, in which her own had remained, she made her way across the drier slabs of stone to a pillar and seated herself in its shadow.

He followed her, reopening his guidebook. "This must be Hadrian's retreat—the Maritime Theater," he said. He sat down on the base of the column, and they held the book between them.

We love to indulge in the generally entertained tradition, and fancy the Emperor Hadrian in his moments of spleen and misanthropy slipping off by himself and recover his spirits from the grievous weight of the care of the empire. . . .

She took off one of her sandals and inspected a blister on her foot. Pulling the strap back over her heel, she glanced at the young man, who was reading carefully. To him, she thought, life was a series of details—a mosaic rather than, say, a painting. He had to have reasons for everything, even if it meant contorting human nature to make it fit into them; so concerned with cause, he ignored consequence. And sometimes, no doubt, it was the right thing. It was the way men's minds worked, she supposed; the process, in fact, by which the world was provided with machines and roads and bridges—and ruins. But they chose to forget that their whole system of logic could be overturned by the gesture of a woman or a child, or by a single line of poetry. This business of reasoning, she reflected, was all very well, within reason, but if one had nothing to be passionate about one might as well be dead.

". . . from the grievous weight of the care of the empire," she read again. They were, very slightly, leaning on each other.

"*Und hier, meine Damen und Herren, war die Zufluchtsstätte des Kaisers,*" said a voice behind them.

There were about a dozen in the group, all with reddened faces under their new straw hats, all with woolen socks under their new sandals, all, she noticed, with cameras and guidebooks. They assembled inside the arch, and made notes as the guide pointed and explained. "*Man nennt es das Wassertheater. . . .*"

The two by the column sat in silence until the group withdrew. Then she clasped her hands around her knees, turning to him. "It's just that you do seem to take yourself rather seriously," she said.

He considered this. "Well . . . in the end, I suppose, one must."

"Exactly. So why begin that way?" But this she said almost as an entreaty, adding: "Anyway, you know, you're so much better than I."

"In what way, for God's sake?"

"Oh, I don't know. Accurate, reliable—"

"It sounds," he remarked, "like an advertisement for a watch."

"*Et ici nous voyons le refuge de l'Empereur*," a new voice announced from the entrance "*On l'appelle le Théâtre Maritime.*"

"Shall we go?" he asked.

Outside, the heat was rising in waves from the plain. The withered countryside enclosing them again, the man and woman crossed a miniature railway that had been laid to carry masonry to and from the works of excavation and restoration. A workman with a paper cone on his head was crushing stones for a new path, using a roller improvised from the broken shaft of a column. They passed from the Large Baths into the Small Baths, and walked along the side of another pool, disturbing the sleep of two or three dusty swans. They found their way into a small museum, where she admired a Venus. ("Her sandals are the same as yours," he said.) Behind the museum, a grooved track took them, through a farm, onto a wooded incline.

It was cooler on the slope. Wild flowers were growing beneath the trees and across the path. Walking in silence, they could hear the birds. The sounds of the plain came to them more remotely, for they were approaching the foot of the mountain; as they reached the first ridge, the white houses and shops of Tivoli could be distinguished, grouped high above the lines of olive trees.

Pausing on the ridge, they kissed—for some unknown reason, as she told herself, still clasped in his arms. She could see over his shoulder the next slope rising, and the next, the black pines lost in thicker vegetation or swept away in areas of cultivation. Her interest in the scene at that moment struck her as ludicrous, and she wondered if he, in his turn, might be studying the countryside behind her head. She drew back, but he kept her hand tightly in his, although the path was too narrow for them both. They were standing quite still, side by side. They might almost, she thought, have been defending one another from two different people.

"We must go back," he said.

There was a washroom near the café, and she combed her hair in front of a scrap of mirror and attended to the sunburn on her face while he selected a table in the garden. An elderly woman in a floral apron brought her a can of cold water, and she washed her feet, sitting on a white wooden chair borrowed from the restaurant. When she took off her sandals, the woman carried them out and brushed them in the garden, and stood watching her while she put them on again.

"Your husband?" the woman asked, smiling and nodding toward the restaurant.

"Yes," she said, because it seemed simpler.

They had a table in the shade. The waitress, moving slowly across the garden, arrived at last beside them and set down their drinks on the cloth. There was a different boy in the bar.

"When I ordered," the man said, "she asked me if we were married."

"What did you tell her?"

He looked surprised. "Why—that we weren't, naturally."

Even under the trees, the heat was intense. She lifted her hands from the table and closed them around the cold glass.

"There's a bus in half an hour," he said. "We should just do it. We may even see it coming down from Tivoli." He thought she seemed tired, but then they had been walking all afternoon. And they hadn't decided anything—although at one point, he remembered, she had told him that it was impossible. She was looking at him, and for a moment he thought he would be able to tell her that nothing else mattered (or whatever it was). But they had walked too far; his head ached slightly from the sun. And now she had turned aside.

CLIFFS OF FALL

"IF you have to be unhappy," Cyril said, "you must admit that there couldn't be a better place for it."

He was speaking to Elizabeth Tchirikoff, who sat on his right at the breakfast table. His wife, Greta, was at his left. They were seated this way, in a row, because the table was on the terrace and commanded across the lake a fine view of the Alps. At their back, past the side of the house, the garden merged into fields and vineyards on the flat green plateau and appeared to stretch, with the interruption of scarcely a single house, to the range of the Jura. On the Jura, this magnificent September, there was no snow whatever. Even on the Alps the snow line was exceptionally high, revealing great jagged precipices of black rock that had seldom seen the sun. Along the lake, the bathing places were still crowded in the afternoons, the weekend traffic was still lethal on the Route Suisse, the tourists still sat outside in the cafés of Geneva. It was weather more majestic, less distracted than summer, and untouched by decay—the improbably fine weather, without evocation or presentiment, that is sometimes arrested in a colored photograph.

Greta looked up warningly at Cyril, but Elizabeth had smiled—as he meant her to—and even made an uncompleted gesture of touching his hand with hers. As if he had set off some small mechanism in her, she made a few more motions with her hands—brushing a wasp away from the strawberry jam and placing the melting butter in the shadow of a loaf of bread—before settling back again in the white wooden chair and closing her eyes against the sun. She had been staying with the Stricklands for three weeks and was very brown, browner than she had ever been in her life. The brown of her breast and back and shoulders fitted exactly to the cut of the blue-and-white striped sun dress she wore almost every day. Her feet were patterned with the lines of sandal straps, and the outline of sunglasses was palely imprinted over her cheekbones. "I feel quite well," she told herself as the sun made circles of yellow and mauve through her eyelids. "If I feel anything, it is that: quite well."

"But then I really don't feel anything," she had told Greta on the day of her arrival, driving back from the Geneva airport. "At the beginning there was the shock, but now I don't feel anything." And when Greta explained in a lowered voice to visitors—the women who came for tea in little pale-blue or gray cars, and the couples who came for dinner—that she was still suffering from the shock ("They had only just been married. He was killed in an accident"), Elizabeth had a sensation of receiving their concern under false pretenses—and of spoiling their visits, since no one could decently enjoy themselves in her presence. For I don't feel anything at all, she told herself. Before leaving New York, she had been given prescriptions for pills that would stimulate her, or calm her, or help her to sleep. In plastic containers, the pills (green and triangular, white and circular, red and cylindrical) lay in a pocket of her suitcase, along with tablets for airsickness and a bottle of cold-water soap. She had not needed any of them.

She opened her eyes a little and looked at the sky, which was now violet, cloudless. A hawk had risen from the pines bordering the road that ran toward the lake; it plunged and soared over the house, dispersing smaller birds, its flight sustained on still, spread wings. It looked, Elizabeth thought, like a child's kite on a string. Will I ever feel anything again, she wondered. Unfeeling, she felt strangely imperiled, as though she might now perpetrate any crime, commit any indiscriminate act, say any unspeakable thing, unless she consciously applied a restraint that had formerly been instinctive—as people who have lost the sense of heat and cold will touch fire and burn themselves, uninhibited by pain.

"There's the postman," said Greta, rising from her chair and wrapping her dressing gown of much-washed turquoise

chenille about her. The postman was coming up the road
—a young boy in a dark uniform and cap tenaciously
weaving his bicycle over the slight incline. Elizabeth sat
up and leaned her elbows on the table, watching him. She
did not herself understand her interest in the mail, which
was delivered twice a day. Nor did she understand why her
interest should make the Stricklands so uneasy; after all,
she thought, they can hardly imagine that I expect a letter
from *him*. The letters addressed to her still expressed
sympathy, enumerated the virtues of the dead, emphasized
the importance of his brief life. Vaguely, she felt a resentment at being left to answer them all—just as, previously,
she had been obliged to acknowledge the letters of good
wishes and congratulation, and the receipt of wedding
presents. Trying to find something different to say for
every one of her short replies, she wondered that the event
did not fully strike her now that it was commemorated in
other people's words and her own. But she wrote, each
time: "Your sympathy has meant so much to me," or, "I
was very touched by your kind letter," not easily but without real pain. Once, she turned her writing pad over and
wrote on the back: "He is dead," and watched the letters
turn fuzzy on the gray cardboard, hoping to comprehend
them. But she remained as numb as before, and after a
moment stroked the words out heavily with her pen so
that they were indistinguishable. If Greta saw it, she told
herself, she would think I had gone out of my mind.

At times, she wondered whether it was simply too soon

for her to miss him. He had been dead little more than a month. Six weeks ago, they had eaten their meals together, made love, driven about in a car. It was no time at all. During his lifetime, they had quite often been parted for several weeks because of his work, and once for almost three months when he had gone on business to the Far East. But she *had* missed him, then. Missed him unbearably, wept at the airport when he set out and again when he came home—thin and exhausted, having been ill and overworked in the Hôtel des Indes or the Raffles or whatever it happened to be. And how, she asked herself, could I have missed him then and not now? Testing herself a little at a time, she found that she could think with equanimity about any aspect of their life together, although she expected continually as she pursued these thoughts that at some point her stillness would be shattered, and grief and anguish would begin.

But the identical days broke, hung suspended, and were absorbed into the green plateau between the Alps and the Jura. Every weekday, and sometimes on Saturday, Cyril walked half a mile to a tiny station overgrown with roses and took the train to Geneva. He worked for an international organization and had a solid-looking office in the Palais des Nations with a view of the gardens. Greta would begin the day with some housework and, at eleven, tea in the kitchen with Elizabeth and the maid, Charlotte. The house had just been built; there were interminable difficulties with newly installed electrical appliances, and a procession of mechanics came to the back door in the mornings on their bicycles—young men with perfect manners and unbelievably high, clear coloring, who lay on the kitchen floor with their heads in the oven, or under the dishwasher, or otherwise obscured according to their particular competence, and were made the object of untimely demonstrations of affection by Aurélien, the Stricklands' spaniel.

Greta and Elizabeth usually lunched on the terrace and sat there in the sun, watching the mechanics and the electricians depart. There was scarcely any traffic on the narrow road, which led only to this house. Occasionally, a farm laborer with that same high coloring, and wearing deep-blue overalls and cap, crossed the fields beyond the garden. Some plowing was going on, discreetly, at a distance. The newly laid lawn that sloped down from the outer edge of the terrace ended in a series of raw garden beds. After lunch, Greta and Elizabeth worked in the garden, bringing fresh black earth from boxes in the garage to cover the exposed clay. Greta worked bareheaded, her coarse black hair pinned up, but Elizabeth wore a straw hat she had found in the closet in her room. Even so, the sun burned through, and when she took the hat off, her brow always showed a red crease and small painful imprints from the rough straw.

At four o'clock, they stopped work and went inside to bathe and dress. Unless visitors were expected to tea, Greta got the car out and they drove to Geneva. In the town they did a little shopping and had *café crème* and pastel-colored cakes outside the Hôtel des Bergues. Tall, delicate women in pretty dresses came and went at the hotel, or walked their small dogs in and out of shops. The avenue along the lake was full of traffic on those beautiful afternoons. Foreign cars drew up at the hotel; elderly men rode slowly past on bicycles, holding limp brief cases over the handlebars. It could be seen from the way in which people drove, or rode, or walked, that everyone was conscious of the weather. Weather was the chief topic of conversation in the café—it was incredible, it wouldn't last, it was warm, it was too warm; the Mont Blanc had been visible every day for a week. No one could recall such a September.

When it was time to pick up Cyril, Greta and Elizabeth took their packages to the car and drove to the Palais. In the stream of people issuing from the main building, Cyril would be the only man without a brief case, the only person without sunglasses. He was not tall; he had blue eyes and receding yellow hair, and a curious rolling walk. ("You are the only human being I know who limps with both legs," Greta had once told him.) His greeting was always the same. "Move over," he would say, as he squashed them into the remainder of the front seat and kissed Greta abruptly on the side of the head. They would sit there, squeezed in the hot car, deciding how to spend the evening. Sometimes they crossed the lake and had dinner in the Old City. Occasionally, they crossed the border into France and dined at the inn of some village in the hills.

More often, they had dinner at home, where they sat at the kitchen table, by the windows, and watched the sun dying in the fields and the Jura flickering with high and lonely lights. They talked all the time. Cyril entertained them with outrageous impressions of bureaucracy, his office having apparently been designed to provide him with a daily supply of absurdities; or he read aloud from the evening paper accounts of the local *crimes passionnels*—a remarkable number of which were apparently committed at the foot of Calvin's statue. Elizabeth got used to the sound of her own laugh, which she had at first found faintly improper. She discovered that she could speak about her life in New York without any awkwardness. If the occasion demanded it, she said "we" or "us" with no hesitation, and in a voice that sounded to her completely natural.

Now, leaning back in her chair at the breakfast table and considering the stability of her emotions as a doctor might survey the course of a fatal disease, she found that her behavior throughout these weeks had been quite normal. I'm a bit odd in the evenings, she conceded, but that's because of the dreams. Since she had come here, she had repeatedly dreamed a stifling, fearful dream of her own death. For that reason, she stayed up long after the Stricklands had gone to bed, reading, or playing the same records over and over again on the phonograph. When at last she went to bed, exhausted, she slept immediately. Each time that she had the dream, she cried out in her sleep and awoke to find the light on and Greta beside her, calling her name. Greta would sit on the bed and take her in her arms, and Elizabeth, unable to speak or weep, pressed her face into the strong, chenille-covered shoulder and trembled. (For months afterward, she could not see turquoise chenille without feeling vaguely reassured.) She did not tell her dream to Greta, from horror and from a kind of shame; she thought that the Stricklands attributed the dreams to grief—and how can it be that, she asked herself, when I never dream of him? When it is not his death I dream of, but my own?

She saw that the Stricklands had put their own concerns aside on her behalf. Their own pleasures, sorrows, quarrels had all been submerged in an effort to help her. She had never felt so protected and consoled. In spite of the calamity that brought her there, the time assumed a simple perfection, so that years later, when she and the Stricklands had become, nonsensically, estranged, that September remained in her memory as something like happiness. It was as if the world had become, briefly, a place where suffering could only occur in dreams, or by accident.

She sat up once more with her elbows on the table and shielded her eyes with her cupped hands. "What shall I put on?" she asked. "Will it be cold?"

It was Saturday, and they were going for a drive in the Alps. Elizabeth was surprised to find herself mildly excited by this prospect. Friends of the Stricklands, Georges and Eugénie Maillard—a short, round, ginger couple who lived in Geneva—were coming over in their car, with a visitor from Paris, at ten o'clock. They would drive together into the mountains and lunch at a restaurant the Maillards had discovered, high up in Savoy. Elizabeth had been in the Alps only once before, in a train. She remembered the long, black tunnels, and the gorges suddenly opening onto Italy. One sees nothing from a train, she thought.

"You'll need a jacket," Greta was saying. "And a sweater. And something for your head. We go so high, you see."

The Maillards led the way, in an ancient Austin. On the other side of the lake, the two cars crossed the border and began climbing into the French Alps. Etienne, the Maillards' friend, sat in the back of the Stricklands' car to keep Elizabeth company. He was a dark, attenuated man who looked like an anarchist (she though, never having seen one). His hair rose into the air above a prominent forehead, his eyes were serious, even sorrowful. He was staying with the Maillards, on his way back to Paris from Italy, to recover from a road accident. A truck had overturned his car on a mountainside near Domodossola. The car, miraculously, had not tumbled into the ravine and he had tried to continue his journey by train. He had, however, been unable to go farther than Geneva.

"It is the shock, you see," he explained. "One doesn't realize. When I first got on the train in Italy, I read a magazine, had my dinner, and so on. But in a little while the tunnels bothered me, and then the sound of the train. By the time we got to Lausanne, I was shaking from head to foot—had a fever of thirty-nine degrees." For Elizabeth's benefit, he added in a solemn aside: "I am speaking in centigrades, of course."

"But that was the same day?" she asked. "The day of the accident?"

"The evening, yes." He looked beyond her, out of the car window. Although they were still far below the snow line, the mountains rose all round them, green and black and peaked with white. Elizabeth, sitting on the side of the car that overlooked the drop, could not see the edge of the road—just tufts of grass, a few inclined shrubs and poplars, and the slit of the valley below.

Etienne gave a short, apologetic laugh. "Hardly the moment to discuss my accident. But, after all, one could as easily be killed on the streets of Geneva—or in an airplane." There was an uneasy silence in the car; Elizabeth's husband had been killed in a plane accident.

Elizabeth stretched her neck to see the road winding ahead, up the mountainside. At an incredible distance, the white peak overhung them. "Can we really get up there?" she asked.

"We can, but we will not," he said. "There's a pass, at about a kilometer, and we take another direction. Does the height trouble you?"

"Not now. It used to, at one time." She spoke as if that were in the remote past rather than a few weeks earlier. "The mountains bother me more—I mean, the look of them."

"The drama," he said. "Yes. Because they have something analogous to our emotions. They look like a graph of one's experience. Isn't that it?"

"I suppose so," she agreed. "There's a poem—

> "O the mind, mind has mountains; cliffs of fall
> Frightful, sheer, no-man-fathomed. Hold them cheap
> May who ne'er hung there."

Having said this, she gave him a sunny smile.

There was a small fox on a long chain in the garden of the restaurant where they stopped for lunch. The house was built on a spur of the mountain projecting into an immense valley and surrounded by shoulders of the Alps. They had lunch sitting on the veranda in the sun, at a long table made of weathered boards, and the fox moved about on the grass below them, just out of reach, clinking his chain and watching them out of bright, despising eyes. There were very few people there, and they were served by the owners of the house, a gentle elderly couple who recognized the Maillards and were pleased that they had returned.

Elizabeth took off her jacket, and then her cardigan, and hung them over the back of a chair. She opened the neck of her blue cotton blouse. She sat on a bench at the table, between Cyril and Etienne. Etienne looked sadder than before and spoke to her in a less natural way, and she assumed that he had, in the meantime, been warned to stay off the subject of accidents. They had pâté and omelets and salad and cheese, and three bottles of wine. The sun moved slowly along the mountains opposite.

"I've never seen the Alps in such weather," Etienne said. "I usually come here in winter." To Elizabeth he added: "You should stay for the skiing."

"Alas, I can't," she answered. "I have to be back at work early in October—I only have six weeks' compassionate leave." It seemed to her, as she said this, an odd excuse to offer for not going skiing.

After lunch, the Stricklands and the Maillards lay down in long green canvas chairs on the veranda and went to sleep, with their faces in the shade. Etienne and Elizabeth leaned on the veranda rail, looking at the mountains and scarcely speaking, and in a while they walked down the steps into the garden. Elizabeth carried her jacket on her arm, and Etienne hung a sweater over his shoulders, the sleeves cross on his chest. In his open shirt and thick, battered corduroy trousers he looked more like an anarchist than ever.

They walked through the garden, the little fox tinkling after them on his chain until he could follow no farther. The same path wound for some distance down the mountain; they could see it grooved through the grass and wild flowers. There were no trees or shrubs on this part of the spur, only the bright-green grass and the tangled flowers. In the great valley, below the black belts of fir trees, a twisting road was lined with fields and farmhouses. Elizabeth kept her eyes lowered to the narrow track on which they walked, pausing now and then to look up at the mountains across the valley. The descent from the track was gradual. The ground sloped away so that the drop, though very steep, was not precipitous. One would probably roll quite a long way, she thought indifferently, before falling into the ravine. She stopped, and Etienne, who was walking behind her, drew level and presented her with a frond of white heather he had picked.

She had nothing to pin it with, but she took it and arranged it in the pocket of her blouse so that it could be seen. She understood that it was the sort of offering a child makes, of the first, valueless thing that comes to hand, to show sympathy. She thought without interest that he was kinder than most people. The sun was in her eyes, and she turned her back to the valley and looked into his face. If he wants to kiss me, he may, she decided. For a moment it seemed almost essential that he should—for surely that, she thought, would shock her into realization; surely *he* (and she could only picture him in a Sunday-school Heaven not much higher than the mountains around them, not much higher than he had been when the plane exploded in the air) would find the means of making his indignation known to her. In the next instant, she was conscious that her head had begun to ache.

Without moving, Etienne had slightly withdrawn. He was no longer looking at her. Perhaps he had not the least desire for her—or perhaps, she told herself with conscious formality, he is respecting my grief. She turned away from him and said: "I don't feel well. Can we go back?"

"It's the altitude," he replied, keeping pace with her and obliging her to take the inward side of the path.

In any case, she thought, I should not let him kiss me—

it would be too disillusioning for him; knowing what has happened to me, he would think there was no loyalty left in the world.

That night she did not dream. She awoke before day-light, feverish and violently ill. Her head still ached. She took aspirin, and was immediately sick again. She lay down on her bed, moaning with pain and confusion, and waited for the night to pass. Her thoughts, although otherwise disconnected, were all concerned with the excursion into the Alps. She saw again, over and over, the thin leaning poplars blowing silently outside the car window, the steep turns of the road, the bright eyes of the fox. In detail, she repeated the descent from the mountain, which had seemed endless at the time, and recalled her own exhausted chat-ter in the car and the strangely anxious face of Etienne. (She considered his anxiety to be without foundation; knowing herself to be a little out of control, she had made a particular effort to behave naturally during the return journey.) More hazily, she remembered coming home and, for the first time, going to bed early. She also remembered that for the first time she had been struck by her solitude when she lay down.

Still, she reflected (as though feeling might attempt to take her unaware), these things have nothing to do with his death; it is all concern for myself. She raised herself on her elbows and hung her head, overwhelmed with nausea. She could hear her own quick breathing; her nightgown clung to her damply about the waist. I am sick, she thought self-pityingly, and closed her eyes. The pain in her head was almost intolerable.

When the wave passed, she lay down again on her side. She stayed this way, quite rigid, for a few moments, and then all at once pressed her face into the pillow, sliding her arm up to encircle her head. She thought suddenly and clearly of her husband, and was surprised to hear her own voice say his name aloud.

The doctor was speaking to Greta in Swiss-German—although, since he practiced in Geneva, he could doubt-less speak French. It is so that I won't understand, Eliza-beth thought without resentment, glad to have this detail explained. Dizziness overcame her again, and when her mind had steadied itself the low voices were speaking French. Greta asked what Elizabeth's temperature was, and the doctor told her. "Of course they are speaking in centigrades," Elizabeth quoted to herself, and smiled. Greta said something about food poisoning. Opening her eyes a little, Elizabeth could see that the doctor's national pride was involved; he was frowning—a slight, blond, youngish man with a rosy Swiss face.

"*En Suisse, Madame,*" he said incredulously, spreading his hands.

Perhaps it would help, Elizabeth thought, if he knew that we lunched in France yesterday. Was it yesterday? Then this was Sunday, unless she had slept through a whole day. She thought she had been given an injection, but perhaps it had only been spoken of—she couldn't be sure that she was not recollecting something in the future. Now they had gone out of the room, and she felt safe in opening her eyes again. The sun, through the gauze curtains, was immoderate, remorseless. Will it go on forever, this weather, she wondered irritably, with an effort putting her hand up to cover her eyes. Will it never rain, never be night, never be winter? If Greta would come, I could ask her to close the shutters. She felt helpless, victimized by the glare. Unwittingly, she had let herself in for all this. She had only meant to marry, settle down, have children—be safe, or a little bored; it came to the same thing. And here, instead, was all this derangement (she felt it, positively, to be his fault)—expense, journeys, illness, and now the sun glaring in at her. All this punishment simply because (she clasped her hand more tightly over her eyelids to shut out the sun) she had loved him. That was it. Because she had loved him.

She sighed. Her arm ached from being raised to her eyes.

"What is it, dear?" said Greta.

"The sun," she explained. "Could you close the shutters?"

"But darling, it's quite dark now."

Elizabeth opened her eyes and found the room in darkness, except for a small lamp on the dressing table. Her hands were folded on the sheet. Greta was holding a tray.

"I can't eat anything," Elizabeth said immediately. The pain had gone from her head. "I feel better, but I can't eat."

"A piece of dry toast."

"No."

"Just tea, then."

"*Please*," she said, almost passionately. Why can't anyone understand, she wondered. She didn't quite know what they should understand—not merely that she should be let alone; rather, a sense of impending catastrophe that rendered absurdly insignificant all this taking of temperatures and bringing of tea. She had no way to describe to them the calamity that was about to befall, no way that would sufficiently prepare them for it. In that respect, it was like her dream.

When she next awoke, the light had returned, but dimly. She thought it must be dawn, but presently she heard Cyril leave for work. When Greta came in, Elizabeth was sitting up in bed. It's still so dark," she said. "It *is* morning, isn't it?"

"It's been raining," Greta told her. She sat down on the bed. "Do lie down. How do you feel?"

"Better," she said. She knew she was no longer sick.

"You look terrible," Greta said, and smiled, and kissed her. "You poor thing. I'll get you some toast and tea."

When she had eaten, she lay down again and began to be aware of the room. There were bookcases facing her bed, all the way up to the ceiling. She decided that there was nothing worse than to be sick in bed with a room full of books; the titles marched back and forth before her eyes. Her attention was repeatedly arrested by the same combinations of color and lettering, or by a design on a book's spine. Hazlitt, Mallarmé, and twenty volumes of Balzac; Dryden and Robert Graves; Cicero and Darwin, and, between them, a brand-new copy of *By Love Possessed*. She closed her eyes, but the cryptic messages, vertical and horizontal, went on transmitting themselves under her eyelids.

She could hear, outside, the faint sound of the plow in the nearby fields. Charlotte was moving the furniture in the living room; one of the accredited mechanics called out from the kitchen. In a little while, there was the ring of the postman's bicycle bell, and the sound of the front door being opened and closed. (Elizabeth was too tired to be interested.) Everything goes on and on, she thought, and did not know whether this reassured or isolated her. It was not, of course, to say that only she had been excluded from the current of life; perhaps others merely conducted themselves better in their exclusion—Charlotte, the mechanics, Greta. Besides, she reminded herself, it's not even as though I were actually suffering; it is only this apprehension that troubles me—the uneasiness I brought down from the mountain.

In the afternoon, she got up and took a bath. The sun had come out, and she lay in a chair on the terrace, wrapped up in a woollen dressing gown of Cyril's and covered with a blanket, because the breeze blowing from the mountains was unexpectedly cool. The sun, too, was not quite so strong, and on the farther shore of the lake— less luxuriantly green today—the neat, opulent villas were slightly veiled. The dog, Aurélien, chased the smaller birds up and down the new lawn, and fled from the larger ones. From time to time, Greta came out of the house to see how Elizabeth was, and once she brought her sewing and sat beside her for a while. They said very little. Greta sat peacefully sewing, occasionally calling the dog away from the birds, or glancing up to smile at Elizabeth. Elizabeth felt bored with her own self-centeredness; she did not know how to stop studying her moods, or even to divert attention from them.

"I must go soon," she said.

"Yes, it's getting colder," Greta said. "I'll just finish this and we'll go in."

"I mean to America."

Greta looked up. "Elizabeth darling, it's only the end of September. Don't think about it for a week or two. You aren't able to go yet. I don't mean because you're sick—I mean because you're . . . not yourself."

She said: "I make no progress."

"Toward what?"

"Toward him," she said.

Elizabeth was allowed to stay up for dinner, which they were to have early on her account. When Cyril came home, he kissed her and, having ascertained that she felt better, declared she had never looked worse. She thought she looked odder than she otherwise might because of her deep tan, which made a curious glaze over her pallor. Her hair hung lankly down on her shoulders in separate dark tails. "I'll wash it tomorrow," she said, pushing it back behind her ears. "If I feel up to it."

They were in the kitchen, Greta standing by the stove and Cyril taking down glasses from a shelf. Elizabeth was sitting, still in Cyril's woollen dressing gown, at the kitchen table, with her back to the window. It was almost fully light, although behind her the sky was reddening and the Jura darkening. Leaning her cheek on her hand, she felt more peaceful than she had all day. With her left hand she made a space for Cyril to put the glasses down among the places laid on the table.

"What would you like to drink?" Cyril asked Greta.

"No," she said absently, stirring the soup. "I mean, not a real drink. Just Perrier—something like that. Put some syrup in it, if there is any."

"Disgusting," he said. He found a bottle of raspberry syrup and made a pink, foaming concoction for her with mineral water. "What an infantile taste," he remarked, setting it down at her elbow. Greta smiled without looking at him, took a long drink, and put the glass down again. She went on placidly stirring.

"What would you like?" Cyril asked Elizabeth, coming back to the table.

"The same," she said. It occurred to her that she had

been thirsty all day. She could hardly take her eyes off the red glass on the stove.

"God," he observed, putting an inch of syrup in a glass and reopening the bottle of Perrier.

"I'm so thirsty," she said. She reached out her hand to take the drink from him.

Greta looked round abruptly. "But, Cyril, what are you doing? She can't have that—she's been sick. Have some sense." She put the spoon down on the stove and looked at him reproachfully. Cyril made a face of comic apology to Elizabeth and turned away with the full glass in his hand.

Elizabeth kept her hand outstretched for a moment longer. Then she withdrew it and propped up her cheek again. The room, the white tabletop, the forks and knives, glasses and plates swam in her tears. The only motion of concealment she made was to turn her face a little into her palm, half covering her mouth. Otherwise, she wept resistlessly and almost silently, without attempting to find her handkerchief or even take her napkin from the table to wipe her eyes. She went on crying—for a long time, or so it seemed—while the Stricklands stood still in the middle of the kitchen, watching her, and not looking in the least astonished that a grown woman should cry because she was refused a glass of raspberry soda.

The sign, high up in the main hall of the airport, was decorated with an enormous cardboard watch and said in English

WELCOME TO GENEVA
PATEK PHILIPPE

"Anyone would think they were expecting some foreign dignitary," said Cyril.

Elizabeth smiled, and put her hand in Greta's. They were sitting on a sofa covered with hard red plastic. Unnerved by the climate of departure, they spoke disjointedly and were rigidly silent when a flight was announced. Elizabeth had buttoned up her black coat and put a scarf around her neck. Like most of the people in the airport, she looked inordinately sunburned for the raw gray day.

"At least, there's no fog," Greta said. "Though the *bise* is still blowing." The drear, chilly wind had gone on for days. "Do you have your pills?"

Elizabeth touched her handbag. "I took one just before we set out. There are only three left, but I'll be able to get more tomorrow."

"I hate the idea of your going back to work."

"It's the best thing, isn't it?"

An elegant woman walked past with a poodle on a leash.

"We should have brought Aurélien," said Greta. "He would have enjoyed it."

Elizabeth felt reconciled to the journey; like someone facing an operation, she only hoped she would behave well. She could not envisage her arrival or make plans for the resumption of her ordinary life. For over a week now, she had been managing to contend with each separate circumstance as it arose, and could look no further. The flight to New York at that time took sixteen hours, and she was ready to be overwhelmed by the prospect. Having taken the pill to stave off the worst of grief, she could not expect to sleep and must spend hours staring, upright, at the sky that was now to be associated with him always.

"*Attention,*" the voice said. They got to their feet, and Cyril picked up her overnight bag. They walked past glass cases filled with clocks and watches, and metal stands stacked with chocolate boxes.

"Would you like something?" Cyril asked her.

"Nothing. Thank you. Really."

"Let me get you some chocolate."

"But they feed you all the time on these planes."

"You never know." When he came back with the package in his hand, she was reminded of Etienne handing her the rough, useless flowers on the mountainside.

At the gate, they embraced her. A young man in uniform examined her passport and her ticket and gave them back to her. She held them in her right hand, with the packet of chocolate. Every action now seemed to her to involve an important and costly effort, as though she were being presented with obstacles which she must continually surmount. Irrationally, she believed that her departure itself represented such an undertaking, and that it would have been possible for her to stay, protected, in the flat green garden between the two lines of mountains without ever fully acknowledging what had brought her there. It was almost like consenting to his death, she thought, walking into the railed enclosure with the other passengers.

WEEKEND

LILIAN, on waking, reached up her arm to pull back the curtain from the window above her bed. The cretonne roses, so recently hung that their folds were still awkward and raw-smelling, tinkled back on brass rings, and sunlight fell around the walls in honey-colored warpings. It was like being under water, she thought, bathed in that delicate light; she had forgotten these contradictions of spring in England—chill, dreary evenings like yesterday's, and bright mornings full of early flowers. She pushed the blankets away and knelt up on the bed to look out the small, paned window. The outer air, the garden glittered; the meadows—for they could hardly be called anything less—unfolded beyond, crowned by a glimpse of the village and the fifteenth-century church. All as suitable, as immaculate as the white window sill on which her elbows rested.

But the room was, of course, cold, and she sank back

into the bedclothes. During the night, she had wakened several times to hear the wind rattling the windowpanes and had pushed herself further down the bed, trying to warm her shoulders. (The little electric radiator had been taken away during the day to dry the baby's washing and had not been returned.) Going to bed last night, she had actually consoled herself with the prospect of departure— that it would be her last night in the house. And tonight, no doubt, back in London, she would wonder about the weekend, and comfort herself by telephoning Julie and by thinking out the long, loving letter she would write when she got back to New York. The letter, in her mind, was already some paragraphs advanced.

Like some desolating childhood disappointment, she thought, this anxiety to get away when she had so longed to come here—so longed to see them, and to see Julie most of all. Because, even though Ben was her own brother, it was to Julie she felt closer; Julie she had missed more in these two years away. Given only this weekend, Lilian felt the need to precipitate confidences—"Are you happy, is this really what you want?" she had almost asked Julie last night, coming upstairs. Which was nonsense, impertinence; one couldn't ask it, and in any case Julie would have laughed and told Ben afterward ("What ever do you think Lilian said to me?"). Married couples always betrayed their friends that way—probably for something to say, being so much together. And Ben, indifferent, would say: "How perfectly extraordinary," or "I'm not in the least surprised," or "Poor old Lilian."

Lilian's room was in the old part of the house—seventeenth-century, Julie had said. Lilian allowed a century either way, for Julie's imprecision and the exaggeration of the estate agent. She lay approving the uneven walls, the heavy beams of the roof, the sturdy irregularities of the window and door. The only furniture other than her bed was a new chest of drawers, a cane chair, and a small, unsteady table. On this table stood a china lamp and *Poets of the Present*, a frayed volume in which Thomas Hardy was heavily represented. The room—in fact, the whole house—looked bare. They needed so many things, Julie had said—practically everything—but for a while nothing more could be done; buying the house had taken every penny. On Friday, when Lilian arrived, Julie had shown her around, walking through the rooms with her hand in the crook of Lilian's arm, separating apologetically at doorways. (All the rooms were at slightly different levels, and there was a step or two at each entrance—sometimes dropping, dangerously, beyond a closed door.) Julie's shy, artless face, lowered so that strands of silky hair drooped on Lilian's shoulder, had seemed tired, frail. Her sweater and skirt were aged, unheeded. Too much for her, Lilian thought, this house, and the baby, though I'm sure it's lovely. "Lovely," she had repeated later, in the nursery, over a mound of blue blanket. In the hallway, it was Lilian who linked their arms again.

She pushed the bedclothes back once more, and lowered her feet to the cold, glossy floor. And Ben, she thought, shivering and resting her elbow on her knee and her chin on her hand. She found it hard to believe in Ben as Julie's husband, Simon's father, a member (as she supposed he must be) of the community, traveling up to London every morning of the week, and at home seeming settled and domestic, reading the evening paper with the air of one who must not be disturbed. She supposed that in his way he must love Julie, but she couldn't really imagine him intimate with anyone. She thought of him as a source of knowledge rather than experience; a good, though not contemporary mind, a person rather than a man.

"I adore you," Ben said, without opening his eyes, "but why are you up so early?"

Julie, at the mirror, uttered a strangled sound. She took a bobby pin from between her teeth and fastened up the last, escaping lock of hair. "I have to take care of Simon until the girl arrives. And think about lunch. . . . And then, there's Lilian."

"What about her?" Ben stretched out into the depression left by Julie's body in the other half of the bed. His eyes, now open, were surprisingly alert. "Come and talk to me."

She came and sat beside him, reaching her arm across his body to rest her hand on the bed. "I just mean I have to think of her—make sure she's not cold or anything."

"Difficult to see how she can be anything else, when we've got both the radiators."

"Oh, Lord! I forgot. . . . *Don't*, darling, after all the trouble I took combing it."

"Why is it done differently?" He loosened another strand.

"I don't know—I suppose because Lilian eyes me as though I should Do Something with myself. She makes me feel that I look . . . *married.*"

"Scarcely astonishing, in the circumstances." He drew her elbow back so that, losing the support of her arm, she collapsed against his breast. She remained there, and he put his arm around her. " 'Old, married, and in despair'— is that the idea?"

"Something like that."

"Too soon for that," he observed, encouragingly. "But I know what you mean. Since she's been here I can hardly read the paper without feeling that I've sold my immortal soul."

Julie giggled. "Don't be awful." She drew away from him and put her hands up to her hair, assessing the damage. "Do you think she's happy? I get the feeling she doesn't *want* anything—you know, doesn't know what she should do with her life. . . ." She opened another bobby pin with her teeth and replaced it at the back of her head. "We, at least know where we are."

" 'I am between water and stone fruit in India,' " declared Ben, looking up at Lilian over the *Times.* "In eleven letters."

"Any clues?"

"None."

"Pondicherry," Lilian said, after a moment's silence.

Ben wrote. Pleased with herself, Lilian curled her legs up on the sofa and wondered if she should be in the kitchen, helping Julie. There were to be guests for lunch.

" 'A secret'—blank—'in the stream.' Tennyson. Nine letters."

"No clues?"

"Begins and ends with 's.' "

"Sweetness," said Julie unexpectedly from the dining room. She appeared for a moment in the doorway and added: "*In Memoriam*," polishing a glass with a dish towel.

"Twenty across," Ben resumed, but Lilian got up and followed Julie.

The kitchen smelled of roasting lamb, and of floor polish and mint sauce. What an appalling stove, Lilian thought; surely they'll replace it.

"Do sit down," Julie told her, pulling out a chair by the table. "We'll be five for lunch—some neighbors called Marchant and the three of us. No, darling, thank you, there's nothing; everything's done. Unless perhaps you'd like to shell the peas." She turned her attention to the meat. "It's quite efficient, really, this kitchen—though, as you see, we had to put in a new stove."

Lilian began to break pods over a colander. "What are they like, your neighbors?"

"The Marchants? We scarcely know them. They drove over one day, in a Volkswagen, to call—we'd been introduced by the previous owners of the house. And they asked us to dinner last week, but we couldn't leave the baby. Seem all right—a bit dull." Having basted the lamb, Julie slid it back into the oven and straightened up. She plunged the basting spoon into suds in the sink. "Nothing against them, really, apart from the car."

Arriving late in their Volkswagen, the Marchants brought with them a big, restless Dalmatian called Spot. Mr. Marchant was stocky and bald, with heavy glasses and a suit of limp tweed. Mrs. Marchant was slight and ginger-haired, and wore a green pullover and a gray flannel skirt. They stood for some minutes in the hall, commenting on improvements in high, authoritative voices, before they could be induced to enter the living room. Mrs. Marchant did not sit down at once, but moved across the room to stare at a picture before veering sharply away to the window. Rather, Lilian could not help thinking, like a small colored fish in an aquarium. Spot after a brisk canter around the furniture, flopped down to pant in a corner, where Ben was preparing drinks.

Mrs. Marchant gave Lilian her divided attention. "You've just been—thank you, with a little water—to America?"

"She lives there," Ben said, stepping over the dog. "Out of the way, Fido."

"Spot," corrected Mrs. Marchant, scenting disparagement.

Mr. Marchant, who was a lawyer, produced some formidably documented views on the conduct of government in the United States. Congressional legislation appeared to him as a series of venal disasters—catalogued, Lilian felt, with a certain satisfaction.

Julie was quietly interrogating the dog, now sitting at her feet. "Are you a good doggie?" Spot smiled, but kept his counsel.

Unable to refute Mr. Marchant, and badly situated for conversation with Spot. Lilian kept silent. Perhaps it's a system, something one gets used to again, she told herself —like doing the *Times* crossword puzzle.

Mrs. Marchant was inclined to be tolerant. "The Americans who come over here seem pleasant enough, don't you think?"

"Oh, absolutely," Ben agreed. He put out his cigarette, and added: "A trifle assiduous, perhaps," before lighting another.

Mrs. Marchant persisted. "But I've always got on well with them. We had four in our house—remember, Hugh? —during the war. Well-behaved boys. They read aloud in the evenings." She nodded to reinforce this surprising memory.

"Did they really?" Julie, who had risen, paused at the door of the dining room. "What?"

Mrs. Marchant's approval diminished. "Well, I *was* hoping for Wordsworth, which Daddy would have so loved—my father was living with us then. But instead they read an interminable thing about a whale—a *whale*, I assure you. I though we'd never see the back of that

147

whale. But mercifully, when the good weather came, they opened the Second Front."

Lilian, glancing up in dismay, was astonished to find Julie's face disarrayed with amusement.

They sat down to lunch, and Ben carved the meat. Spot, having found his way under the table, squeezed back and forth among their legs, his firm, bristly sides heaving with cheerful interest, his tail slapping wildly. Julie looked pained, and once laid down her knife and fork as though she were about to speak—but didn't. At last Mr. Marchant got up from the table, apologizing, and called the dog to the door.

"Out, damned Spot," he said, pointing. Everyone laughed except Mrs. Marchant, who had heard the joke a hundred times. The dog pattered out as if he had intended this all along.

Julie washed the dishes, and Lilian dried them. The Marchants, waving, had disappeared with Spot in their car, shortly after lunch. Ben had gone out to work in the garden ("Before the rain comes," Julie said, although there was no sign of rain). In the sun outside the kitchen window, Simon slept in his pram.

"Is he warm enough there?" Lilian asked.

Julie looked up, her hands in the sink. "Oh, don't you think so?" she asked anxiously, alarming Lilian, who had expected a confident reassurance.

"It's beginning to get chilly," she said. Together, they

looked uncertainly at the strip of sunshine on the grass
Their shoulders touched.

"Oh, God!" shouted Ben from the garden. He crossed
rapidly in front of the kitchen window and came in at the
back door, a bundle of drooping plants in his hands.
"Julia," he said, using her full name to emphasize his displeasure. (How infantile men are, Lilian thought.) "Julia,
the lupines are all dug up. Will you please tell those people
for Christ's sake not to bring their filthy dog here again?"

"Yes, dear," Julie replied seriously, apparently memoriz-
ing the message in order to convey it with complete ac-
curacy. "Can't they be replanted?"

He shook his head. "The blighter's chewed them."

Lilian wiped the draining board and hung the wet dish
towel on a rod to dry. "I'll bring Simon in, shall I?" she
said smoothly, and made her way past Ben into the garden.

"Leave the pram," Julie called. "Ben will bring it."

Outside the kitchen door, the grass was sparse and
trampled, and flaked with wood shavings from the recent
passage and unpacking of furniture. Beyond, however, it
became lavishly green, in need of cutting and scattered
with spring flowers. The garden, more delicate than ever
in the already dying light, was surrounded by ancient trees
and, on one side, by a thick, trim hedge of box. A memory
even as one stands here, Lilian thought, saddened by an-
ticipation of her own nostalgia—and yet pleased all at once
to have come out at this moment, to find the scene im-
posing some sort of misty symmetry on the untidy events

of the day. I may cry, she told herself with surprise, as she lifted the sleeping Simon.

Ben, still grasping the ravished lupines, looked at her with interest as he came out of the house.

Lilian gathered up the trailing blanket with her free hand and walked slowly away. He will say: "Poor old Lilian," after I've left, she reminded herself. In the kitchen, she handed Simon over to his mother. "Now I must really go and pack," she said.

Lilian leaned from the window of the train. "I'll telephone you from London," she told Julie.

It will come right again, on the telephone, they assured each other silently.

Julie, suddenly pale and tired, brushed away tears. "It's cold. I should have brought a coat."

"What?"

"It's cold."

"Next time I'll come in the summer."

Crying, Julie laughed. "It'll still be cold. But come back soon."

"Do you have everything you need?" Ben asked, too late for ambiguity, glancing at the magazine stall.

"Yes, thanks. Oh, goodbye." The train drew away. "Goodbye!"

"Goodbye! Lilian . . . goodbye."

They waved, close at last for a moment, before the train ran into the darkness.

The two on the platform stood still for a few seconds, convalescent, before they walked away to their little car. In the clear, black, country air outside the station, Julie shivered again. The wind had risen, as it had the night before. They got into the car without speaking. Only when the engine started, on the third try, did Julie move up against Ben. He put his arm briefly around her, and then withdrew it. The car moved off.

"Poor old Lilian," Julie said.

HAROLD

EVERY evening of the summer, lanterns were hung from
the oleanders and they had dinner in the garden. The table
was a long and rickety affair on trestles, and there were
always insects because of the lights, but on balance it was
worth it. The evenings were cool even after the August
days, which recorded heat, long after dark, in the villa's
outer walls. The wall facing onto this terrace-garden was
still warm to the touch, although it was past nine o'clock
and Signora Ricciardi and her guests were sitting down to
dinner.

The scene, too, was worth the discomfort: the white
table, three flasks of wine, pale dishes of bread, red dishes
of meat, green bowls of salad; the summer-colored dresses
of the women, and a crimson shawl hung on a chair; everything scented by flower beds, in eclipse beyond the lanterns, and by lemon trees, which stood about in great stone
urns. Above the line of hills facing across a valley, the

sky glowed from the lights of Siena, but the house at night rode its hilltop in rolling, dark countryside with the purposeful isolation of a ship at sea, and people around the table, too, assumed something of the serene animation of voyagers.

Bernard Tourner was as lean and astringent as his wife, Monique, was plump and soft—a dove in her gray dress. For many years they had come from Paris to spend their summers at this *pensione*, and each morning they would disappear in their little ancient car for an excursion to Arezzo or Volterra, or simply into the Chianti hills, returning as children return from a trip to the seaside, refreshed and exhausted and painfully sunburned.

Bernard's appearance was an index of his personality, sensitive and slightly waspish. A quick understanding and a rich, ready memory made him an excellent companion at the table, but because of his occasional moodiness it was felt that Monique was not to be envied. However, they were deeply dependent upon each other, and Monique seemed always sweetly and unheroically content.

They were sitting, this evening, on either side of Charles Holmes, who was an Englishman, and who, from shyness, talked and listened with a habitual vagueness, glancing at Dora, his wife, sitting opposite. Dora passed the wine to him across the table; Dora was dark and beautiful and not shy at all.

"O *pittore*," called Signora Ricciardi, from the head of the table. Charles turned to her, always charmed that she should address him in this way, since he was an amateur and not very gifted painter, on holiday from a business concerned with lead and zinc. "O *pittore*, have you seen our three boys at all? Have they come back yet?"

Charles gestured toward the house, as if to conjure up the three young men, who at that moment came hurriedly into the garden and seated themselves at the table, murmuring apologies. Englishly alike in grave manners and incisive speech, in an almost womanish refinement of feature and fair skin reddened but not tanned by the sun, they had the names of antique Romans: Julian, Adrian, Antony. With quiet fortitude they had received, that summer, telegrams confirming success in their examinations at Cambridge. At twenty, they already offered a certain distinction and the promise of charm. The only criticism that might have been made of them was that their background and prospects had been provided so amply as to encroach a little on the scope of the present; nothing had been left to chance—perhaps on the assumption that chance is a detrimental element. "*Tutto a posto*," the Signora said of them.

In her way, the Signora herself was as much "in place" as these boys; she would never have been mistaken for a voyager. Sitting at the end of the table, a slender, ageless woman with a disproportionate share of accomplishments, she chatted and rejoiced and sympathized with her guests, sharing their confidences and fulfilling their expectations, giving them a sense of infinite leisure, as though these symmetrical days of summer were to last forever. Their recollections of the villa would be almost indistinguishable from memories of her.

A little withdrawn from the talk that evening, she was listening for the arrival of a pair of unknown guests, a mother and son who were the friends of a friend. All day they had been expected—a not unwelcome intrusion into the intimacy of the present guests, who had been in one another's company all summer. Though, indeed, it had all gone very well this year: no one had been ill or quarreled or fallen in love. They were all on the best of terms, even with Miss Nicholson.

Miss Nicholson was a diminutive middle-aged English-woman who played—surprisingly—the cello and was attending the summer courses at the music academy in Siena. She did not attempt even the simplest of Italian phrases, and she spoke of England with a longing as constant as though she had been condemned to exile. Most surprising of all, she wore a hat to the lunch table, a navy-blue sailor hat with a group of white flowers at one side of it, and in this hat she would take the bus to Siena every afternoon to attend her lesson. The small, prim figure burdened with the cello had become familiar in the spiraling main street that led to the academy, and the instrument was recognized as a token of sympathy and permanence, the antithesis of the camera usually carried by foreigners.

The boys were at their best with Miss Nicholson, who represented a type familiar to their own family circles.

They were kind and deferential, invariably willing to help with the inevitable cello or to find out where she could buy an English newspaper. In return, she regarded them with real affection and an almost personal pride.

Now, as the meal began, the arrival of the new guests was announced by one of the maids, the smiling, circular Assunta. "*O Signora,*" she said, the formal vocative "O" of Tuscany coming oddly from that genial face, "*son appena arrivati da Firenze.*" Arriving at Siena by the late train, the new guests had come out to the villa in a taxi and were seeing to the unloading of their luggage. The Signora, taking up her red shawl, went into the house to greet them, and around the table there was a short, expectant silence.

"*Una vecchia signora,*" whispered Assunta, handing around the *pasta,* "*e un giovane grande.*" Two chairs were added to the table and two more places set. Conversation resumed, but now they were all detached, awaiting this diversion.

Presently a voice could be heard, raised as a voice sometimes is in a strange house, and the Signora brought the new guests through the doors that led from the living room into the garden; the two women were followed by the "*giovane grande,*" a tall young man who remained in shadow behind them while introductions were made. The men rose from the table, scraping their chairs over pebbles.

The mother, large and handsome, was of that vigorous type of Englishwoman generally caricatured for its addic-

tion to outdoor life. Gray hair, squarely cut, contributed
to the strength of a face almost grimly straightforward, a
directness scarcely modified by an impression of unhappiness. She was wearing a dress of brown linen much creased
across the lap from the train journey and, around her neck,
a heavy pendant of Mexican design. On her arm was a
silver bracelet of incongruous delicacy, and Florence had
contributed the sandals in which her feet were firmly
planted apart.

Names were pronounced and mispronounced to her by
the Signora, and she smiled politely, repeating them like
a lesson. She was led to the place laid for her next to Bernard and settled into it.

Her son's name was Harold. He stepped forward into the
circle of light to be introduced and stood silent while
chairs were shuffled along the table to accommodate him.
The three boys, now reseated, looked him over with cour-
teous reserve, exercising that perception for affinities and
failings with which public-school life had endowed them.

This boy had none of their diffident grace. Long-limbed
and excruciatingly awkward, he was still, at their age, almost grotesquely adolescent. He was very brown, and
dressed in khaki trousers and a blue shirt with rolled
sleeves, and scratches on his arms were blotched with that
purple antiseptic upon which British mothers place such
reliance. His blond hair and eyebrows, sun-bleached to a
startling fairness, contributed to a look of vacancy that
really began at wide-spaced, wide-staring eyes. On his be-

half, certainly, there would be no telegraphed confirmation of outstanding performance in examinations; rather, one imagined an education interspersed with letters from school principals, sympathetic and unyielding: "Harold's gifts are not suited to the discipline of the school curriculum."

Stumbling to his chair with an embarrassed acknowledgment of greetings, he sat down next to Dora. His mother was already embarked on an easy tide of conversation concerned with her journey. "So hot in Florence . . . a little tired, yes, but what a beautiful journey . . . light most of the way . . . Lovely country . . ."

Bernard was helping her to *pasta*. "Yes, it's a journey one never tires of, that trip from Florence to Siena."

"So much to see," she went on. "That scenery, sometimes vast and sometimes almost in miniature, like a fairy tale. . . . A great fortress quite near here, what would that be?"

"That was probably Monteriggioni," replied Bernard. "It's from the thirteenth century. But Tuscany is crowded with these hilltop fortresses and walled towns."

"Tomorrow you will see another, just below the house," the Signora told her. "Montacuto. It was ruined by Barbarossa."

"So hard to associate violence with this countryside," the new guest said, and sighed, comforted by antiquity.

"It isn't all as remote as that," the Signora said. "In the last war the front passed through here. The Germans were in this house."

158

"You see how it is," said Bernard, with a faint smile. "In this country everything has been *done*, as it were— even this landscape has been done to the point where one becomes a detail in a canvas. And they all know too much. In Italy one is almost too much at ease, too well understood; all summer here I feel that nothing new can happen, nothing can surprise or call our capacities into question; that none of us can *add* anything."

"Does this mean we shan't see you here next year?" asked Dora, laughing because Bernard had come there for so many years.

Bernard laughed, too. "Well, you English, you find a sort of prodigality here, too—an easy acceptance which you enjoy but which, after all, you don't wish to emulate."

"You mean that we have scruples about giving but none about receiving?" Charles asked.

"Not even that," Bernard said. "I simply mean that in our countries one must still be prepared for a few surprises, but here all experience is repetition, and that gives one an outrageous sense of proportion. That's why we feel so comfortable—why we find it so attractive to come here. After all, France is certainly as beautiful as this"—Bernard included the Italian peninsula in a brief gesture.

"And England," said Miss Nicholson, misunderstanding.

"Well, it isn't a competition, after all," replied Charles, filling her wineglass. "Do you know France, Miss Nicholson?"

Miss Nicholson replied that she did not, adding that she had been there several times.

The new guest remarked that she knew France well but that this was her first visit to Italy, and took the opportunity to resume her account of it. Yes, Florence was lovely, lovely, but a week was nothing, one must go back. "There is too much, far too much," she added accusingly. With a forkful of salad she indicated infinite riches.

"And you." Dora turned to the boy beside her. "What did you think of Florence?"

He stared at her uneasily, shifting his feet on the pebbles beneath the table. His mother's face clouded with a recognizable intensification of the discontent already seen there. "He scarcely saw anything of Florence," she said. "He wouldn't even have seen the cathedral if I hadn't insisted on it."

"I had to do some work," he murmured.

His mother appealed to the table. "Such an opportunity at his age. One would think he'd make the most of it." She gave the three boys a covetous, comparing look. Disconcerted, they vaguely protested their own inertia, not wishing to appear to advantage.

"I'm determined that he shall see Siena properly," she persisted.

Something in this prospect seemed to dishearten the boy even further, and he went on with his meal. He did not look at his mother. While she chatted on again about Florence—the heat, the della Robbias, the bargains in tooled leather—she directed toward him a current of censure and disappointment, evoking from him a slow, painful awareness.

But for the wondering eyes, the boy's expression would have been intense. It was a look that concentrated hard but could not quite find its object. Once or twice he entered the conversation, to express agreement with an enthusiasm suggesting that he seldom found his views shared, or to disagree with an emphasis which confirmed that impression. Between times, he maintained a state of subdued apology for his outbursts; in fact, apology appeared to be for him an involuntary means of self-expression. "I'm sorry," he said, passing dishes or reaching his daubed arm for the salt; "I'm sorry," as his wineglass was refilled. His self-effacement was, in its way, demanding; his youth, his gaucheness called up a collective effort of reassurance and encouragement, but he, in a sense, was proving the stronger character. As the evening drew on, his ineptitude pervaded them all.

Signora Ricciardi always left the table early, to negotiate with the cook the meals for the following day. At this interruption, Harold's mother rose, too, tired from her long day, and nodded around the table. "Don't stay up late," she told Harold, who stood to wish her good night. "You know how tired you are."

This knowledge passively acquired, Harold prepared to hurry with his fruit. Dispelling a momentary, hopeful silence, the other guests encouraged him to stay, describing to him the house and its surroundings, proposing excursions into the town. They listed for him the attractions of Siena, from *pinacoteca* to post office, and he listened diligently, leaning forward and twisting his napkin about his fingers. He was taking them and their attentions very seriously, almost as seriously as he took himself. A burden of compulsory activities could be seen mounting in his imagination, although he might easily have guessed that those hot days would dwindle into a catalogue of churches unvisited and pictures unsurveyed. At last, with an effort, he mentioned anxiously that he intended to keep part of the day free for his work.

"You must be studying?" asked Dora.

"No, no, I'm not studying anything now."

"What is your work then?"

"I mean my writing."

"Writing?"

More vulnerable than ever, he glanced around the table. He was repeating a familiar experience.

"I mean poetry. Well . . . yes, poems."

Into the silence Miss Nicholson said gently: "Well, I hope you will read them to us."

He raised his eyes toward her with his concentrating, round-eyed look, not doubting her word. "I have them here, upstairs," he said.

The evening seemed to have lost its balance. They allowed him to fetch his poems, feeling the extent of their indulgence and a sense of imposition. They were already inventing to themselves noncommittal expressions of interest and wondering how soon they might stop him. Their manners preventing an exchange of glances, the three boys smiled down at their plates, comfortably appalled;

they were all at once drawn together, dissociated from so flagrant a breach of regulations. It was entirely possible that they also wrote poetry, but only within the bounds of a fastidious reticence. Charles Holmes pushed back his chair a little to stretch his legs and muttered: "Let him read one, then—just one. I'm ready for bed."

The boy came out of the house again, clutching a bundle of papers. When he placed them on the table, they slid outward—single, scribbled pages of all sizes. Seated, he examined them, rustling through an apprehensive silence. He read to himself for a moment, and his audience suddenly saw that he was no longer intensely aware of them, or, indeed, of himself, and that his face was unrecognizably calm. Even his arm, resting on the table's edge, was curved toward the papers in a controlled and easy gesture. They were slowly troubled by an idea that formed among them. Without looking about, each knew, too, that it had occurred to the others: an idea almost to be repudiated, requiring, as it did, so much accommodation.

When he had read aloud for a few minutes, the boy looked up, not for commendation but simply to rest his eyes. Charles said quickly: "Go on." The inclined young face had grown, in the most literal sense, self-possessed. Their approval, so greatly required in another context, had now no importance for him. He spoke as though for himself, distinctly but without emotion, hesitating in order to decipher corrections, scattering his crumpled papers on the table as he discarded them. It seemed that no one moved, although the three boys no longer held identical positions; they had separated into solitary, reflective attitudes that conceded this unlikely triumph.

Assunta came to remove the last dishes, but left, after a moment, without disturbing them. A moth thudded against one of the colored lanterns. The evening was at its best, cool and clear. From time to time, his voice tiring, the boy paused to shuffle his papers, or he made some brief explanatory comment on the subject of a poem before reading it. When someone asked whether this was all recent work—as though it could possibly have been otherwise—he replied that it had all been written in the last year or two. "There are more all the time," he said, and laid his hand on the shaggy papers as if they had taken him by surprise.

The wall overlooking them suddenly broke open at a square of light, shutters clattering back against stone, and Harold's mother leaned from the window. Framed in ivy tendrils, she presented, in metal curlers and a dark dressing gown, an altered version of that type of post card in which ringleted maidens used to lean toward one over window sills. The boy stared up at her blankly, his eyes emptied of all impression. Without looking at the others, she reminded him that he had traveled all day and that it was almost one o'clock. The wall was abruptly resealed.

Harold continued to look up for a moment, and it could be seen rather than heard that he muttered: "I'm sorry."

He began to put his papers together, at first slowly, and then quickly and nervously, picking up pages that fluttered to the ground. His authority relinquished without a struggle, he rose from the table holding the bundle insecurely against him. "Good night . . . thanks awfully . . . good night," he said, and disappeared into the house with his ungainly steps.

Presently they heard a sound like a splash, a sound that could only be his papers falling across the tiled floor of the living room. They gave him time to gather them up, convinced that alone there in the half darkness he was saying: "I'm sorry."

THE PICNIC

IT was like Nettie, Clem thought, to wear a dress like that to a picnic and to spill something on it. His wife, May, was wearing shorts and a plaid shirt, and here was Nettie in a dress that showed her white arms and shoulders—and, as she bent over the wine stain, her bosom; a dress with a green design of grapes and vine leaves. He could tell, too, that she had been to the hairdresser yesterday, or even this morning before setting out to visit them. She hadn't changed at all. Unrealistic, that was the word for Nettie. . . . But the word, suggesting laughter and extravagance, unexpectedly gave him pleasure. Feeling as though Nettie herself had cheated him of his judgment, he turned away from her and glanced down the hillside to where May was playing catch with Ivor, their youngest boy.

If May had left them alone deliberately, as he assumed she had—and he honored that generosity in her—she was mistaken in thinking they had anything to say to one another. They had been sitting for some minutes in complete silence, Nettie repacking the remains of the lunch into the picnic basket or, since the accident with the wine, fiddling with her dress. But what could two people talk about after ten years (for it must be getting on to that)? Nettie, though quite chatty throughout lunch, certainly hadn't said much since. Perhaps she expected him to mention all that business; it would fit in with her sentimental ideas. Naturally, he had no intention of doing anything of the kind—why bring up something that happened at least ten years ago and made all three of them miserable enough, God knows, at the time? Yes, that would be Nettie all over, wanting to be told that he had often thought about her, had never forgotten her, never would—although whole months passed sometimes when Nettie never entered his head, and he was sure it must be the same way for her; at least, he presumed so. Even then, he would remember her only because someone else—May, perhaps—spoke of her.

In fact, it was because someone else brought her to his attention that the thing had come about in the first place. He had not, in the beginning, thought her attractive—a young cousin of May's who came to the house for weekends in the summer. He had scarcely noticed her until a casual visitor, the wife of one of his partners, spoke about her. A beautiful woman, she had called her—the phrase struck him all the more because he or May would have said, at most, a pretty girl. And Nettie, that day, had been dressed in a crumpled yellow cotton, he remembered—

found his life quite dull and could rejoice that, after all, she had not shared it. (He saw himself, for an instant, with what he imagined to be her eyes. What a pity she had come just now—he had worked hard last winter, and he thought it had told on him.)

It was true, of course, that he had responsibilities, couldn't be rushing about the world pleasing himself, as she could. But no man, he assured himself irritably, could be entirely satisfied with what had happened to him. There must always be the things one had chosen not to do. One couldn't explore every possibility—one didn't have a thousand years. In the end, what was important? One's experience, one's ideas, what one read; some taste, understanding. He had his three sons, his work, his friends, this house. There was Matt, his eldest boy, who was so promising. (Then he recalled that during lunch today he had spoken sharply to Matt over something or other, and Nettie had laughed. She had made a flippant remark about impatience; that he hadn't changed at all, was that it? Some such silly, proprietary thing—which he had answered, briefly, with dignity. He knew himself to be extremely patient.)

Yes, Nettie could be quite tiresome, he remembered— almost with relief, having feared, for a moment, his own sentimentality. She made excessive demands on people; her talk was full of exaggerations. She had no sense of proportion, none whatever—and wasn't that exactly the thing one looked for in a woman? And she took a positive pride in condoning certain kinds of conduct, because they demonstrated weaknesses similar to her own. She was not fastidious, as May was.

That was it, of course. He had in his marriage the thing they would never have managed together, Nettie and he— a sort of perserverance, a persistent understanding. Where would Nettie have found strength for the unremitting concessions of daily life? She was precipitated from delight to lamentation without logical sequence, as though life were too short; she must cram everything in and perhaps sort it out later. (He rather imagined, from the look of things, that the sorting process had been postponed indefinitely.) For her, all experience was dramatic, every love eternal. Whereas he could only look on a love affair, now, as a displacement, not just of his habits—though that, too —but of his intelligence. Of the mind itself. Being in love was, like pain, an indignity, a reducing thing. So nearly did it seem in retrospect a form of insanity, the odd thing to him was that it should be considered normal.

Not that it wasn't exciting in its own way, Nettie's ardor, her very irresponsibility. It was what had fascinated him at the time, no doubt. And she was easily amused— though that was one of her drawbacks; she laughed at men, and naturally they felt it. Even when she had been, so to speak, in love with him, he had sometimes felt she had laughed at him, too.

In all events, his marriage had survived Nettie's attractions, whatever they were. It was not easy, of course. In contrast to Nettie, May assumed too many burdens. Where Nettie was impetuous and inconsiderate, May was scrupulous and methodical. He was often concerned about May. She worried, almost with passion (he surprised himself with the word), over human untidiness, civic affairs, the international situation. He was willing to bet that the international situation never crossed Nettie's mind. May had a horror of disorder—"Let's get organized," she would say, faced with a picnic, a dinner party; faced with life itself. If his marriage lacked romance, which would scarcely be astonishing after twenty years, it was more securely established on respect and affection. There were times, he knew, when May still needed him intensely, but their relations were so carefully balanced that he was finding it more and more difficult to detect the moment of appeal.

He felt a sudden hatred for Nettie, and for this silence of hers that prejudiced one's affections and one's principles. She tried—he could feel it; it was to salve her own pride—to make him consider himself fettered, diminished, a shore from which the wave of life receded. And what had *she* achieved, after all, that she should question the purpose of his existence? He didn't know much about her life these past few years—which alone showed there couldn't be much to learn. A brief, impossible marriage, a lot of trips, and some flighty jobs. What did she have to show for all this time—without children, no longer young, sitting there preoccupied with a stain on her dress? She couldn't suggest that he was to blame for the turn her life had taken—she wasn't all *that* unjust. She had suffered at the time, no doubt, but it was so long ago. They couldn't begin now to accuse or vindicate one another. That was why it was much better not to open the subject at all, actually. He glanced severely at her, restraining her recriminations. But she had lost her mocking, judicial air. She was still looking down, though less attentively. Her hands were folded over her knee.

Well, she *was* beautiful; he would have noticed it even if it had never been pointed out to him. . . . All at once he wanted to say "I have often thought of you" (for it was true, he realized now; he thought of her every day). Abruptly, he looked away. At the foot of the hill, May had stopped playing with the children and was sitting on a rock. It is my own decision, he reminded himself, that Nettie isn't mine, that I haven't seen her in all these years. And the knowledge, though not completely gratifying, gave him a sense of integrity and self-denial, so that when he looked at her again it was without desire, and he told himself, I have grown.

He has aged, Nettie thought. Just now, looking into his face—which was, curiously, more familiar to her than anyone else's—she had found nothing to stir her. One might say that he was faded, as one would say it of a woman. He would soon be fifty. He had a fretful, touchy air about him. During lunch, when she had laughed at his impatience, he had replied primly (here in her mind she pulled a long, solemn, comic face): "I have my faults, I suppose, like everyone else." And like everyone else, she noted, he was willing to admit the general probability so long as no specific instance was brought to his attention. He made little announcements about himself, too, protesting his tolerance, his sincerity. "I am a sensitive person," he had declared, absolutely out of the blue (something, anyway, that no truly sensitive person would say). He was so cautious—anyone would think he had a thousand years to live and didn't need to invite experience. And while, of course, any marriage must involve compromise (and who, indeed, would know that better than she?), that was no reason for Clem and May to behave toward one another like a couple of . . . civil servants.

She could acknowledge his intelligence. And he had always been a very competent person. Wrecked on a desert island, for instance (one of her favorite criteria), he would have known what to do. But life demanded more, after all, than the ability to build a fire without matches, or recognize the breadfruit tree on sight. And one could hardly choose to be wrecked simply in order to have an opportunity for demonstrating such accomplishments.

Strange that he should have aged like this in so short a time—it would be precisely eight years in June since they parted. It was still a thing she couldn't bring herself to think of, the sort of thing people had in mind when they said, not quite laughing, that they wouldn't want their youth over again. Oddly enough, it was the beginning, not the end, that didn't bear thinking about. One weekend, they had stopped at a bar, in the country, on the way to this house. It was summer, and their drinks came with long plastic sticks in them. Clem had picked up one of the sticks and traced the outline of her fingers, lying flat on the Formica tabletop. They had not said anything at all, then, but she had known simply because he did that. Even now, the thought of his drawing that ridiculous plastic stick around her fingers was inexpressibly touching.

Naturally, she didn't imagine poor old Clem had planned an affair in advance, but even at the time she had felt he was ready for something of the kind—that she was the first person he happened to notice. For the fact was that they were not really suited to one another, which he would have discovered if he had ever tried to understand her properly. He had no idea of what she was like, none whatever. To this day, she was sure, he thought her trivial, almost frivolous. (And she was actually an acutely sensitive person.) No wonder they found nothing to say to one another now.

It *was* a strain, however, their being alone like this. And how like May to have arranged it this way, how ostentatiously forbearing. Magnanimous, Clem would have called it (solemn again), but May had a way, Nettie felt, of being magnanimous, as it were, at one's expense. Still, what did it matter? Since they had invited her, after she had run into May in a shop one afternoon, she could hardly have refused to come. In an hour or two it would be over; she need never come again.

It did matter. It wouldn't be over, really. Her life was associated with Clem's, however little he might mean to

her now, and she must always be different because she had
known him. She wasn't saying that he was responsible for
the pattern of her life—she wasn't that unjust. It was,
rather, that he cropped up, uninvited, in her thoughts almost every day. She found herself wondering over and
over again what he would think of things that happened
to her, or wanting to tell him a story that would amuse
him. And surely that is the sense, she thought, in which
one might say that love is eternal. She was pleased when
people spoke well of him in her hearing—and yet resentful,
because she had no part, now, in his good qualities. And
when she heard small accusations against him, she wondered whether she should contest them. But, for all she
knew, they might be justified. That was the trouble with
experience; it taught you that most people were capable
of anything, so that loyalty was never quite on firm ground
—or, rather, became a matter of pardoning offenses instead of denying their existence.

She sympathized with his attitude. It was tempting to
confine oneself to what one could cope with. And one
couldn't cope with love. (In her experience, at any rate, it
had always got out of hand.) But, after all, it was the only
state in which one could consider oneself normal; which
engaged all one's capacities, rather than just those developed by necessity—or shipwreck. One never realized how
much was lacking until one fell in love again, because love
—like pain, actually—couldn't be properly remembered
or conveyed.

How sad it was. Looking into his face just now, finding

nothing of interest, she had been so pierced by sadness that tears filled her eyes and she had to bend over the stain on her dress to hide her face. It was absurd that they should face each other this way—antagonistically, in silence—simply because they had once been so close. She would have done anything for him. Even though she no longer cared for him, saw his weakness quite clearly, still she would do anything for him. She cared for him, now, less than for any man she knew, and yet she would have done anything. . . . It *was* a pity about her dress, though —wine was absolutely the worst thing; it would never come out.

Upright on her rock, May gave a short, exhausted sigh. She closed her eyes for a moment, to clear them, and Ivor called out to her that she must watch him, watch the game. She looked back at him without smiling. On either side, her palms were pressed hard against the stone.

THE WORST MOMENT
OF THE DAY

"THIS is the worst moment of the day," said Daniele.

The table—with the emptied wine flasks, the grapes and figs left in large bowls, the clusters of stained napkins—was like a beach from which the tide had ebbed. Conversation had dwindled until slow afternoon sounds could be heard through shutters striped with heat.

The long room had windows at each end, and on one side opened through double doors into the drawing room. The opposite wall, slate blue, was bare except for two paintings hung together like illuminations on a blank page. They were landscapes painted by Marina some years ago, before she and her brother turned the villa into a *pensione* and her time ceased to be her own. She sat at the head of the table, straight and slender in a faded green dress, red-gold hair falling on her shoulders. Her hands were loosely clasped in her lap, and in her face poetry and reason met without the customary signs of struggle. She turned toward her brother's remark with a faint smile.

As though at a signal, the diners drew themselves together to surmount this worst of moments. Chairs scraped, a glass was knocked over; some inconclusive suggestion was made for a drive down to Florence in the evening.

It was late in the season, and the four guests—an elderly English couple and a young one—stood around the table as singly as the surviving fruits lay in the china dishes. Old Mr. Fenwick, who had been at the villa just a week, pushed his chair back into place and crossed to the windows. Unlatching one of the shutters, he peered into the garden, and only his wife's going over to join him suppressed his daily utterance concerning a brisk walk. There was something of fearful symmetry about the Fenwicks, he slim and inflexible, she plump and stately. It was their first journey to Italy, and they had been gratified to find so many forebodings justified.

Through the slit that now parted the shutters, the old man stared despondently at the day. The scene, it was true, was of dimensions comparable to those of his own land—in fact, he had made the comparison all too frequently, as though Tuscany were remarkable only for this similarity—but then there was that sky. He had never experienced such a sky. In England, where heaven is a low-hung, personal affair, thoroughly identified with the King James Version, a sky such as this would not have been tolerated for a moment. It was a high, pagan explosion of a sky, promising indulgence for all kinds of offenses to which he had not the slightest inclination. He felt, beneath it, exposed and ridiculed. And the light, too—a light that not only illuminated but was an element in itself, as distinct as rain . . . He would go and read in his room, after all, for he realized that the brisk walk, if taken, would be somehow impeded by that dazzling light.

The younger couple, the Stapletons, lingered at the table, folding their napkins. The Stapletons had spent other summers at the villa, but this year, for the first time, they had brought with them some unconfided anxiety of their London life. Francis, a fair man with a sensitive and orderly manner, contrived to conceal his present unhappiness—or at least to give it a reasonable, disciplined air that made it socially presentable. But his wife, Harriet, carried her part of their suffering publicly, and in return received, unfairly, a greater deference.

Marina had begun to stack the dishes for the maids, who had their lunch at this hour. "*Vai riposarti, cara,*" she told Harriet, drawing the napkin out of her hand.

After a moment, Harriet did go—but not, immediately, to rest. She disappeared into the drawing room, and they heard the opening creak of the side door and the thud of its closing. Francis was helping Marina to clear the table, walking around it to bring her the littered fruit plates. It was a relief to him to be here, in this cool room, doing automatic tasks, but he knew that in a moment he must go and look for his wife. He took a tray from the sideboard and arranged on it the glasses gathered together by Marina. Marina, who seemed to know everything—and he found it rather shocking that with her secluded life she should know so much—stood silent, pushing the grape seeds onto one large dish with a knife and making a pile of the stained plates beside her, but he felt soothed and understood, as if she had said something to console him. He dropped the napkins into their basket and, with a murmured excuse, left the room.

In the drawing room, he recovered his book and reading glasses—placed on the table when the lunch bell rang— and opened one of the shuttered doors into the garden. The door was weighted with the heat that met him as he stepped outside; it fell heavily back into place behind him. It annoyed him that Harriet should go out at a time when all other people—all of Italy—rested; annoyed him that he was unable to turn his annoyance into anything but concern, for real anger might have alleviated his misery. He made his way around to the front of the house, his mind presenting his predicament to him in words so simple that they might, but for the context, have been uttered by a child: "She does not love me any more."

Then: "She loves someone else." But if that was so, why were they here, together, trying to make things work again? He brushed with his shoulder the dying fronds of wisteria at the corner of the house, and stood in the wall's shadow, looking for Harriet.

In front of the house was a formal garden, and from this a crescent of graded steps descended to an avenue of ilex. The short avenue was never used now, the house

having been connected with the road by a separate, grav-
eled drive that led to the kitchen door. The trees, which
needed trimming, met overhead and stood deep in weeds
and wild flowers. Throughout the day, hens wandered into
the avenue and picked among the straggling grass and
made their way haltingly up the steps to stare into the
ordered garden. From time to time, on the road below, a
car passed, going toward Florence, and country sounds
reached the house from the surrounding slopes.

Harriet sat now on the lowest of the arc of steps, her
back curved in the sun, her face pressed into her arms,
which were folded on her drawn-up knees. The sleeves of
her pink blouse had been rolled up, and her skin was moist
with heat. Her cotton skirt was carelessly bunched under
her. She was motionless, not even roused by the hens
rustling near her feet.

Her attitude was so abject, so forlorn, that Francis, at
the top of the steps, stood quite still before he called her
name. "Harriet."

The face she raised to him, however, was smooth and
preoccupied, only creased above the eyes by the pressure
of a bracelet. He came slowly down, dropping from step
to step, and sat just above her, his knee touching her
shoulder. She put no weight on him. After a moment, she
resumed her former position without speaking.

He opened his book at the beginning and shaded the
print with his hand. He had had a shock, coming upon her
like that. And her calm uplifted face had not reassured

him—because what was shocking, he thought as he turned the first page, was that it had seemed perfectly plausible that she, who had been chattering pleasantly enough at the lunch table a few minutes before, might have come out here and thrown herself down in this abandoned attitude in real anguish. It would have been terrible to find her so, but not surprising; people in general, and he and she in particular, were so separate that anything was possible. That knowledge moved him to press his knee once more against her bent shoulder. Feeling, perhaps, that some response was required of her, she turned her cheek toward him, her eyes closed.

"Hens are ghastly," she observed. And then: "Read me something."

He read aloud the lines he had just reached:

> "... *Ferme les portes*
> *Il est plus facile de mourir que d'aimer.*"

"Heavens," she said, and turned her face back into her arms.

He closed the book and put it on the stone step beside him. He looked down at her huddled body and dark, shaggy head, her brown arms and exposed knees, the tail of her blouse, which had come out of her skirt. He parted the hair on her neck and laid his hand there. "Come inside," he said. "We can't stay out in this heat."

She tilted her head once more. "In a moment," she replied.

"No," he insisted. "Really. It's the worst part of the day."

"In a moment," she repeated, wishing he would take his hand, which had become quite damp, off her neck. One can't ask to be left alone, she thought, or not to be touched, even once in a great while, without creating a scene—without changing everything. Do we have anything in common at all, she wondered—almost idly, because the sun had drained her. Will we manage it? Sometimes it is all right. But not today.

She sat up straight, thrusting her hair back from her forehead. He rose and helped her to her feet. She brushed at her skirt and made a perfunctory effort to push her blouse back in at the waist. They went up the steps together.

The hallway was cool and darkened and smelled strongly of the carnations that stood, white and red, in a big ceramic jar on the marble table. The stairs, which were of white stone, projected from a wall of colossal depth, so that, climbing them, one imagined oneself scaling a cliff. The house had been intended for pleasure, and perhaps that was why it was built like a fortress.

The Stapletons' room also was in darkness, for the maids had closed the shutters throughout the house. When Harriet opened them, it seemed that heat, no less than light, filled the room, igniting the red stone tiles, the pale walls, the two narrow white beds and their ornaments of brass. Below the window, as she looked down, a garden enclosed

by a tall hedge of ilex was brilliant, too, a square of olean-
der, phlox, and petunias. Descending softly from the house,
the country rose again into a freshly plowed hillside and
a skyline black-penciled with cypresses.

She lay down on her bed. Francis came and sat beside
her on the edge of the bed, filling her vision. She moved
her head toward him on the pillow without rising, like a
sick person. She had spoiled his tranquil, costly summer.
Too much was wrong between them for these fine days
to be enjoyed, or this idyllic place. They did not blame each
other, having been educated since the days when faults
could be attributed; nevertheless, it seemed that the sense
of grievance was very strong. It was the worst moment of
the day—an inarticulate exchange of pain. She could not
speak yet, or make promises, and in any case the reassur-
ances she could give were too meager to offer. Detached,
she pitied him, too, and saw that she had never been more
dear than now, when she lay there excluding him with her
indifference and her look of displeasure. On her knee, his
fingers became points of heat through the light cotton skirt.

"All right?" he asked, helplessly.

"I thought I might sleep."

"Shall we go down to town before dinner?"

"See how we feel. After I've rested, I may take a walk."
And, to forestall him: "I'll be back in time to go in to
town."

He rose and pulled one of the shutters, so that her face
was shielded from sunlight. With indignation and longing,

he felt disqualified from kissing her as he turned to leave.
It was almost as if he did not dare to.

"If I were you," she said, elaborating their estrangement,
"If I were you, I should have a look at the car before we
go."

Pondering the discomfort of having hurt her husband
and the relief afforded by his departure, Harriet folded
her hands across her breast. Somewhere, one of the maids
was ironing, her soft singing accompanied by the thump
and clash of the iron. Down at the road, a dog and a scooter
barked together through the roar of a truck climbing the
hill; a woman called; a child cried out.

Harriet stared at the ceiling, the physical displacement
of her sorrow expanding within her—difficulty of respi-
ration, and an aching in ears and eyes. She wondered if
this were, after all, the worst moment of the day, and
thought of the scene in the kitchen every morning when
the letters came. (It was the butcher who brought the
mail from Florence once a day; his small gray delivery car
trundled up the drive about eleven o'clock. Occasionally
he was late. There was talk with the maids before the
bundle was laid down, with the day's meat, on the kitchen
table, and there were papers, circulars, letters to be turned
over before Harriet could be sure that there was nothing
for her. Sometimes there was an envelope with an English
stamp, and for a moment anxiety would be replaced by
apprehension—for what could now be written that she
might want to read?)

She knew she must not weep, and she watched the ceiling with the same impassive face and dry eyes she had turned to her husband in the garden. It seemed to her that the tears were flowing inside her head.

The wheel of her mind turned laboriously on a familiar route, as though a required number of revolutions might set it in easy motion. The ray of sunlight lay flat on the farthest wall, patterned by the vines about the window frame. The house at this hour became a well of greenish light filtered through the color of it shutters. From time to time, a cicada droned from the garden, pressing upon the silence a weight that seemed to seal it completely. The afternoon swung Harriet, immobilized, between sleeping and waking, and slowly closed on the distraction of pain.

When Francis came downstairs, he found Marina preparing to go into the garden.

"It's all right," she told him, lifting her hand a little to check his protest. "I'm going to tie up one or two plants and come straight back." There had been a storm the night before.

He followed her into the garden, feeling rather like a child with whom other children will not play, and who is allowed, for that reason, to trail about after the grownups.

Marina put her implements down by a bed of dahlias and drew on a pair of blackened gardening gloves. She knelt to examine the fallen plants, and after a moment looked up at Francis, shielding her eyes from the sun with her gloved hand. "The sticks," she said. "Would you mind? In the shed at the back of the house. But not the short ones," she called as he turned away. "The long ones, in the corner near the door."

Francis walked down the path, the sun pressing on his head and shoulders. The dim shed, smelling of earth and fertilizers, was cool after the garden. In the corner near the door were a hoe, a rake, a stack of pots, and an encrusted trowel. The only sticks he could find, on a shelf, were too short for Marina's purpose, but after a hasty search in the half darkness he took them back into the garden.

Marina did not hear him return, and he stood looking at her as she bent over the plants. All her actions were complete and reassuring, all her attitudes graceful and yielding. As she worked, she watched her own hands with a reflective smile, and her hair fell forward across her cheek and swung with the movements of her arms. It occurred to Francis that he had never been so close to beauty. His need for deliverance, for human comfort, was so great that for a moment he thought he had actually taken Marina in his arms, and could feel under his fingers the worn material of her dress and the delicate bones of her shoulders.

"Oh, Marina." He fell on his knees beside her, his hands still full of the sticks from the shed. "Marina."

She looked up abruptly. Kneeling, they stared at each other.

His eyes dazzled. He lifted his closed hands. "I could only find the small sticks."

She was very pale. For an instant, he could imagine how she might look if she were ever to lose her composure.

She sat back on her heels. "They must be there," she said. "I'll go and look." She got up and left him on his knees on the grass, his hands extended and full of short, blunt sticks.

Mr. Fenwick, at his window, was relieved to see the young man get up and come inside; the sun was downright dangerous. Surely the summer should be over by now, even here, he expostulated to himself. He would have expostulated to Mrs. Fenwick, but a deep, regular breathing from the bed promised him little response. She had taken off her shoes and lain down to sleep, with a scented handkerchief on her forehead, as soon as they came upstairs from lunch. But Mr. Fenwick maintained, at the window, something approaching a vigil, holding his book (Trollope: *Phineas Finn*) firmly on his knee. Someone must, after all, keep their wits about them.

When he saw Francis leave the garden, Daniele closed and latched his shutters and sat down in an armchair. He propped his feet on the end of the bed and laid his open book (Ausonius: *Mosella*) upside down in his lap. Marina asks for this, he told himself—invites confidences, implies sympathy, and then isn't prepared to go through with it.

She is as incapable of living, of truly living, as I, he conceded—with a suggestion of high praise. She likes to preside serenely over the emotions of others, but she doesn't care to participate. And those who do participate seem shrill or untidy by comparison.

This wave of resentment, subsiding, was replaced by an image, as true as if he had risen to confirm it from the window, of Marina alone in the garden in the heat, patiently restoring the dahlias.

Still, he continued to himself (effortlessly, because he considered these things almost every afternoon), we *are* unreal. We shall never do anything now except go on here, feeling the extent of our losses. We've been obsolete since . . . (Here he left in his mind the row of dots that stood for Fascism, the war, debts, the last illness of his father, the death of Marina's husband, who had had a heart attack in 1949 while hanging a painting in his house in Milan—matters now too familiar to cause pain or merit reiteration.)

On the other hand, he concluded, Harriet and Francis —exasperating as they may be at the moment—are *real.* He pictured Harriet intrepidly hailing a London bus or standing in a crowded room with a glass in her hand. (He himself never entered a shop or made a new acquaintance without reluctance and apprehension.) And there was something admirable about being close enough to love to be able to quarrel over it. The thought of Harriet, now, lying tormented on her bed—crying, possibly—because of love, filled him with wonder and envy.

He turned his book over and switched on the lamp at his side.

Lying on her back with her eyes closed, Harriet reached out her arm for the little traveling clock, lifted it onto her chest, and held it there, too sleepy to look at it. It rose and fell on her breastbone for a few moments, and then tumbled forward with a glassy slap.

Raising the clock before her face, she opened her eyes. "Five past four," she announced. She put the clock back on the table and looked about the room. On the wall, the sunlight seemed less certain now, the design of leaves a little blurred. "Yes?" she called, in answer to a knock on her door.

Marina came into the room and leaned on the high brass rail at the end of the bed. Harriet once again had the sensation of being treated as an invalid, and sat up, cross-legged, smoothing her skirt over her knees. "You've changed your dress," she said.

"I got muddy from gardening," Marina explained.

"You shouldn't have gone out in the sun," Harriet said, with satisfaction.

"It did me no harm. Did you sleep? I came to ask if you would come down for tea." Tea, unexpectedly, was always precisely that—thin, hot tea in chipped cups, uncompromised by cakes or biscuits.

"Is it really time for tea?" Harriet glanced again at the clock. "I thought the afternoon would never end. Didn't you?"

Marina straightened her back and smiled. "Every afternoon of the summer, I have serious doubts of the evening," she said. "No amount of repetition reassures me." She released the brass bar of the bed. "I must go and see if Daniele wants tea."

Harriet lowered a foot to the floor, feeling for her sandals, and promised to come downstairs. But as the door closed, she crossed the room and, resting her hands on the window sill, looked again into the garden. The light was the easier light of late afternoon. Farther along the wall, between the columns of the loggia, geraniums were fluttered by a faint breeze. On a nearby hill, a bell was rung—an unmelodious, useful country bell. Two little barefoot girls in faded pink dresses and straw hats were carrying to the kitchen a basket of zucchini for the evening meal. Each held a handle, and the tilting basket was covered by the golden flowers of the plant; these would be fried tomorrow for the lunch table.

Harriet turned to the mirror, where a face glimmered in the glass, shadowed by tousled hair. She would go and look for Francis, with some atoning suggestion for a walk together. Oppressed by obligation, she leaned her elbows on the bureau and heard him calling her somewhere in the house. Inaudibly and mechanically, she answered him. "Yes, dear."

The endearment was disconcertingly sharp, but she looked again into the glass and, as his steps drew near, slowly began to comb her hair.